The Weirdness of Leesome Shrouds

The Weirdness of Leesome Shrouds

M. A. Hunt

First published in Great Britain in 2012
Balaclava Publishing, 36 Langham Street, London, W1W 7AP

Copyright © M. A. Hunt 2012
Cover illustration copyright © L. Crebbin 2012

The moral right of the author has been asserted
A CIP catalogue record for this book is available from the British Library.

ISBN 978-0-9573569-0-0 (Paperback)
ISBN 978-0-9573569-1-7 (Hardback)
ISBN 978-0-9573569-2-4 (epub)
ISBN 978-0-9573569-3-1 (mobi)

Prepared and printed by York Publishing Services Ltd

www.balaclavapublishing.com

to

the screwed up ear ...

Thank you

-Chapter One-

THE DEPARTURE

An eerie breeze crept along the platform causing the Victorian train station clock to creak. George Price felt a shiver sneak down his neck as the chill of darkness lurked all round. He jumped as a crisp packet scratched its way along the ground behind him.

He shook his head. 'Get a grip, you're 13, not three.'

George looked over to the other platform. Where was everyone? He looked at his watch, then up at the clock.

'*Aw, no way!*'

The clocks had gone back an hour.

'*Dad!* You could have reminded me. I'm an hour early. That's great! Just great! What am I going to do now?'

Turning around he caught a bleary reflection of himself in a window. He ran his fingers through his thick brown hair. That new hairdresser's on the high street had done a really good job, he would definitely go there again.

A scraping from over to his left demanded his attention. Slowly he turned to see what it was, or *who* it was.

Nothing there, just some rusty old lift doors. *Strange* though – he'd never noticed them before, and he'd walked along here hundreds of times. Yet there was something about them, something almost familiar. Why though? He walked over and stared at them for a short while. There were some lift buttons at the side. They looked as though they might fall apart if he pushed them, but he tried anyway. Nothing happened. He noticed that the doors were open slightly so he pressed his eye right up to the gap, it was dark inside but he could just about manage to see. There was an old fashioned light bulb hanging from the ceiling. He shuddered as it started to swing, and then realised that it was just that breeze again. But there was something else swaying in the corner, something dark and ghostlike. He squinted. Ugh, cobwebs, a mass of tangled cobwebs. That was it, he'd seen enough.

But wait – hang on a minute, there was something on the lift floor. A parcel of some sort.

George put his fingers between the doors to pull them apart. It was tough but he managed it. Soon there was enough of a gap to squeeze through and get to the secrecy within. He stepped onto the sagging floor and moved cautiously towards the waxy brown paper parcel, all the while keeping one eye on the cobwebs. Particles of dust rose up, powdering the bottom of his jeans and fogging the floor. Wafting away the dust, he bent down to pick up the parcel.

He stumbled backwards. *The parcel* was addressed to *him*.

No way!

He looked again. Yes it definitely had his name on it. But it couldn't be, he was dreaming – right?

George pinched himself on the cheek. OK, not dreaming. But a parcel for him? Unreal. But how? Why?

That scraping again. Quickly he turned around. The lift doors were closing!

'OH NO!'

George rushed to get to the doors, but it was too late, the gap was too narrow to get even his foot through. He heard a click as the doors sealed him in. He stood still for a moment in the blackness listening to his heart freaking out, and daring only to move his eyes.

Then he threw himself at the doors and bashed them full force with the sides of his fists. He pummelled, pushed, pulled and scratched, until his shredded fingers and battered hands could stand no more.

'*Come on! Open up!*' he screamed.

He kicked the doors hard, fleetingly imagining the scuffmarks he would be leaving on his new trainers.

But still the lift doors wouldn't open.

He screamed out for help until his throat became sore and his head felt like it would shatter. Then he remembered that there was no one around yet. He was all alone.

Goose bumps prickled his skin and a cold shiver slithered way down inside him.

A high-pitched crackle came from above as the old light bulb that had been swinging in the breeze was illuminated. George's brown eyes squinted up at the soft light.

What was going on now?

Nothing. Silence.

'Think!' he shouted, slapping the palm of his hand onto his forehead. 'Just get yourself together and think.'

He took six deep, but shaky breaths. He checked his watch.

Yeah, that was it. It wouldn't be long now. People would be coming for the train soon – in half an hour. Then he could shout out – someone would hear him and come to help him – he was sure of it – wasn't he?

But for now he would just have to wait. His jittering legs shook him down into the furthest corner and darkest point of the lift. He sighed and shook his head. He stared over at the parcel and decided to take a look, after all it *was* addressed to him. He leaned over, picked it up and holding it up against his ear he shook it gently; dust clouded his shoulder. Soundless.

Then the faint smell of something sweet, like faded roses, perfume maybe. His mind suddenly flashed back to a time he tried not to think of too often – when his mum had come into his room *that* evening six long years ago. She'd wiped the hair off his face and kissed him on the forehead. 'Goodbye,' was all she'd said as she tiptoed away, closing the door quietly behind her.

That was the day she'd left them – him and Dad – no explanations – no apologies – not even a note – just a permanent kiss *goodbye*. George felt anger and disappointment flush his face as he remembered the packed bag he'd seen in the hallway the night before, and her telling him that she was going on a little break and that she'd be back in a week's time. But she had never come back. What had *he* done so wrong back then that had driven her away like that? He'd tried to tell himself that it wasn't his fault she'd left, but deep down he knew he could never be sure of that. One thing he did know for sure though, was that even if he wasn't to blame, whatever way he looked at it, his mum had made his life unbearable, and she'd done it on purpose.

As the weeks passed his dad had gone into a deep depression, and the laughter that once existed at home was replaced by one great big silence, and an overwhelming sense of sadness crept into George's life, one that he just couldn't shift, and one that he never managed *to* shift. Day after day he would come home from school and watch Dad staring into his microwaved meal, stirring and prodding the food, seldom eating. And day after day George began to sink into a frustrated depression, that week after week turned into a desperate anger towards his dad. He despised his selfishness, his weakness, after all George had lost her too, and needed Dad now more than ever. He just wished that Dad would shout about it, scream about it, just anything, anything at all other than the endless silence.

At night George would curl up in bed and stare at the outline of the light from the hallway for hours, waiting, hoping, that

Dad would come into his room to comfort him, to talk to him about how much they both missed her, to just let him know that he cared. But the nights passed slowly by, and Dad never, never in all the years once came.

Then the worst. It was just two weeks before Christmas that the rumours began, vicious rumours that spread through the village like a spilled pint of blood on a white floor. Rumours that made everyone in school stare, whisper, taunt him, call him vile names. Even some of those he thought were his good friends joined in, it seemed everyone, everyone except his two best friends Onion and Big Toe. They'd stood by him unquestionably, always defending him against those horrendous rumours – disgusting rumours that George couldn't, even now, bear to think about. And the reason he couldn't bear to think about them, the reason he felt so very sick when he did, was because after a while, he'd started to believe them himself.

Abruptly his thoughts jolted back to his present situation, and wiping the sweat from his face he glared around at the lift walls. He jerked his head up to check the spider situation, then down at the parcel that lay unopened on his knee. He needed something to take his mind from his thoughts, so quickly he picked it up, untied the purple ribbon that bound it together and ripped back the outer wrappings. There was definitely something in there. But what was it? He reached in and took hold of it, it didn't feel very exciting. George pulled it out.

Just a timetable. *Boring!*

But hang on a minute.

A *lift* timetable?

George flicked through the discoloured pages.

OUTBOUND LIFT TIMES 2012

	Oct 27th	Mar 30th
Middlebridge	05.15hrs	06.15hrs
Guillotine Place		
Bleeding Rivers		07.32hrs
Leesome Shrouds	18.38hrs	19.48hrs
Murderley Edge	21.46hrs	22.56hrs
The Domain of Morgue		03.16hrs
Helcrix (end of line)	06.66hrs	

What did it all mean?

The only place he recognised was Middlebridge.

He looked through the rest of the booklet. He shook his head, he didn't get it. Why would a lift have a timetable? Trains and buses had timetables. Oh, and school! Not lifts, or escalators, or anything like that. This was stupid.

Now what else was in the parcel? George quickly tore away some more of the paper. He could see something, he snatched it out. A box of pills? He turned it over, the prescription sticker on the box had his name on it. George shook his head.

'Now you've really got to be joking?'

GEORGE PRICE

SICKNESS TABLETS

TAKE ONE TO FOUR TABLETS A DAY DEPENDING ON THE

LEVEL OF SICKNESS YOU REQUIRE.

(Distributed by; Aspirations Apothecary)

Take with or directly after a meal.

Warning – contains 300mg Queasy-nalystaline.

Why would he ever want to take tablets to make himself sick? To get better, yeah – sick, never! This was crazy! Something really weird was going on!

He popped one of the pills out of the foil wrapper. It was a sickish, dark green colour. 'Ugh gross!'

He put both the timetable and the pills into his pocket and tore away the remainder of the parcel. There was one more box. It was long and thin, and quite heavy. He read the writing on the box. His eyes stretched open.

'NO WAY!'

*****'Not seeing is believing!' *Bleeding Rivers' Evening Chronicle.* AGE 11+

® THE INVISIBLE TORCH.

The Invisible Factory™   Includes batteries.

With trembling fingers George fumbled about with the box until he could see the contents. He gawped at the silvery torch. 'Aw no way – this isn't invisible.' He tipped the torch out of the box into the palm of his hand, he tried the switch – no – he shook the torch gently and tried again. Then he checked to see that the batteries were correctly installed. Still nothing.

'Rubbish – all of it!'

Still shaking his head he put the torch into his pocket, alongside all the other useless objects. Then thinking about everything that had happened that morning, a shocking thought exploded in his head. Completely flustered, he delved into his fully lined jacket pocket and pulled out the lift timetable. He needed to check something. A few of the pages ripped apart as George forced his way through the booklet, until he found the page he was searching for.

He looked at the date of the outgoing lift – it was October 27th – today's date. He checked his watch.

'OH NO!'

If this timetable was correct, then this lift would be leaving Middlebridge in precisely four minutes.

For the next two minutes George paced up and down the lift, panting, occasionally punching and often kicking the doors.

By the third minute George collapsed to the ground in a tight ball, clutching his aching head and piercing his scalp with his fingernails.

One minute.

He grasped his face with his rigid hands and stared through liquid eyes as the second hand on his watch ticked to 05.15hrs.

The final tick – a rumbling – *beneath him.*

Jumping to his feet he seized hold of the rusty handrail on the wall of the lift with his sweating palms. The lift began to shake as if wanting to break itself apart. A rush of blood surged through George's contracting veins as a mass of bitter, stagnant air assaulted him. The lift began to twist and plummet, first in one direction, then in another. George tightened his grip on the handrail as his feet left the ground and his body collided against the sides of the lift. He felt no pain. Swirling memories from his past hurtfully invaded his mind, and consciousness began to slip away. Through clouded visibility George watched his deadening fingers depart from the handrail.

STOP!

The lift ceased to fall.

George shook his head in distrust as the lift began to go up – quite peacefully, and steadily.

What the hell was happening now?

The lift jerked still. The light bulb crackled again, only this time the light was extinguished. Alone in the blackness George listened to his hammering heart.

PING!

The lift doors opened. Light streamed in, and George dived out.

-Chapter Two-

UMPTEEN TIB LANE

George picked himself up off the floor and dazedly looked around. Where was he? This wasn't the station. And why was it light here? He rubbed his eyes. Opening them again he took a proper look all about him. He frowned at the narrow lanes, the cobbles, the crouched buildings, and the unfamiliarity of everything. Then he looked up at the *sandy* coloured sky. A hollow coldness soared through George's body. And then he knew – he knew for sure, that there was no way this was Middlebridge.

An all too recognisable scraping came from behind. George turned around just in time to watch the lift doors closing again. He leapt over, but once again he was too late. The doors were strong and determined – they shut him out! And just as he thought things couldn't get any worse, the stone wall in which the lift was situated began to shift and fold, until there was no evidence of any lift having ever been there at all.

'NO! NO! NO! This isn't happening!'

And although deep down he knew it was probably useless, George reached up and beat and battered the sides of his already bleeding fists fast onto the bleak stone. But breathlessness and weariness came all too quickly and as he dropped his arms and dipped his head he cringed at the redness oozing from his hands. He pulled a tissue out from his pocket and wiped away some of the blood. The stinging was so real he started to believe that it really wasn't a dream. But surely there was no way this kind of thing happened in real life – did it?

George walked around the back of the stark building in search of a way of getting back inside – but there were no windows – no doors – no way in. He walked around at least a dozen times, and then, *an idea*. Frantically he reached into his pocket again and pulled out the lift timetable. He thumbed his way through the booklet – pages quivering.

'Next lift home. Come on. *Come on!* Where are you? Oh no... *NO. Please NO!*'

George screwed up the timetable and collapsed back onto the wall, his back scraping him down to the ground.

'TWO weeks?'

He buried his face in his hands.

'Oh God. What am I going to do? Stuck *here* for two weeks.'

He swallowed, very slowly. But where was *here*? It could be anywhere. What if he was in *Hell*? That *was* the direction the lift went, down – and down – and still further down. The teachers at school were always saying that bad people went to Hell, and although he hadn't always been that bad, he knew he hadn't been that good either.

He began to shiver – then a sudden realisation. Of course, it couldn't be Hell – it wasn't hot enough. Hell was boiling hot. It was quite cold here – in fact he was really cold. Then he supposed he could be dead; he felt as though he could be. His body felt completely wrecked.

No not dead, he couldn't be dead – please!

His head jolted upwards as he took in a sharp breath. Jerking his head from side to side he dragged himself up the wall by his elbows. Of course he wasn't dead, he was alive, he could feel pain. But think – what to do now? That was it, he should try his phone. He took it out of his pocket – no signal – he hadn't really expected anything else. He looked all around at the warren of narrow lanes. An enormous, grey-brown cloud cast a leeching shadow, chilling him to the core. He watched as the darkness trickled along the lane in front of him, behind him, to his side, all around him. He needed to make a decision and quick, and before it got dark. He needed to find someone, someone to ask for directions back to Middlebridge. He decided to go down the street that was the least murky. Passing a large white building on his left he briefly wondered whether or not he should knock. He decided against it, not for any particular reason – a decision he would later regret.

Striding down the various streets George began to wonder whether anyone lived here at all. He shuddered as the dark grey houses began to loom upon him, so he quickened his pace, feeling the humid air smother his skin and dampen his clothes. He turned down a snicket, passing a sign – Tib Lane. Lots of narrow houses lined the street on both sides, orange light beams forcing themselves out through pinched windows, and a wispy haze haunted the blackened chimney stacks.

A plate on the gate of the first house announced that it was number 17. He peered over the gate and into the house; the windows were dirty and the curtains dark and worn. He passed it by, not at all feeling inclined to knock. Number 18 was a tall thin house, daunting in its manner; no he wouldn't try there. *Come on, you need to knock somewhere, just do it.* He decided that he would knock on the next one, whether he liked it or not. He walked straight up to the gate. A plaque read, Umpteen Tib Lane. He almost smiled as he pushed open the gate and walked up to the front door. It was small and red, with a huge brass knocker. Deep breath, three firm knocks should do it. George could hear the sound of footsteps approaching on the other side. He wanted to run.

A boy at the door, about his age with short blonde hair, a stripe of freckles across his face and a wide grin. George was glad it was someone so friendly looking.

'Hi I'm George.'

'Er yeah, can I help you?' said the boy not so smiley now.

'Hope so,' said George. 'I, I – er...' He didn't know what to say.

The boy looked him up and down. 'Are you alright?'

George shrugged. 'Yeah, suppose.'

'You sure, you look... well like death. And what've you done to your hands, they're a right mess?'

'I – er – just caught them on something, it's nothing, really.' George began to fidget. 'Look something's happened, something really weird, and I've ended up here.'

'So you're not from around here then?'

'No.'

'Thought you had a weird accent. Peter by the way.'

George thought his was peculiar too. 'Oh yeah, hi there, Peter.'

'So you were saying...'

'Oh yeah, I'm er – I'm.' What to say? 'Well I'm from a place called Middlebridge. You heard of it?'

'Nope.'

Just what he'd expected. 'Thought you were going to say that. Where exactly am I?'

'Are you trying to be funny?'

'No. Look I know this is going to sound mad, but well I'm sort of – well sort of lost.'

'Lost? What do you mean lost?'

'Well lost, but not the way people usually get lost.'

Peter just stared.

'Can you just tell me where I am, I mean the name of this place?'

'You're joking right? Has Molly put you up to this to get me back for that *swearing syrup* I slipped in her drink last night?'

'No. Honestly. No one's put me up to this. I just really don't have a clue where I am.'

'Well, you're in Leesome Shrouds.'

A strangeness crept through George's body reaching deep inside. He shivered. 'That's it, I've had it!'

'You what?'

George decided to tell him everything; he knew it was going to sound unbelievable – and it was, but what choice did he have? 'OK I'll explain.'

When George had finished telling Peter precisely what had happened to him Peter just smirked. 'That's an amazing story George, it really is, but I have to say I don't believe a word of it. Now I know it's Molly, or it could be that Brian Bones getting me back. Mind you it could be Eddie Flannagan or...'

George cut him short. 'Peter, I'm not making it up, I swear I'm telling you the truth.'

Peter said nothing, just stared at him.

'I know it sounds crazy but, oh I don't know, I don't know anything any more. I just need someone's help.'

'OK! OK!' said Peter, eyeing him suspiciously. 'If it's true, then tell me where this lift is?'

'It's about five minutes away. That way, and around there, but it's not there any more.'

'Yeah, right.'

'It isn't. When I turned around the walls just kind of moved all around it, and then – well, it was like it had never even been there. There was just an old grey building, no windows, no doors, nothing.'

For the first time Peter looked slightly interested. 'Over that way you say?'

'Yeah. Do you know where I mean?' asked George.

'No windows, no doors?'

'Yeah, that's it.'

'That's the Banishing Block,' said Peter.

'What is it?'

'Don't know. No one knows, no one knows what's inside, no one's ever been inside, or if they have they've never come out. It's called the Banishing Block because of the stories of people that have disappeared in through the walls. Banished forever – ghosts maybe – ghosts from Helcrix.'

'Helcrix?' said George. 'Helcrix? I know that name? Why do I know that name? What is it?'

Peter pointed to the ground. 'A place, way, way down there. You really don't want to go there.'

'That's it! I know that name because it's on the lift timetable,' said George. He reached into his pocket and pulled out the screwed up timetable. 'Look – here!'

Peter took hold of the timetable. 'Where did you get this?'

'It was in the lift. It's got the times of the lift in it. Look, it says there isn't another lift back to Middlebridge for two weeks.'

Peter flicked through the timetable.

'If there isn't another lift for that long what am I going to do?'

'Is this for real?'

'Yeah,' said George. 'I told you, it's all mad isn't it?'

'You could say that,' said Peter. 'One of the maddest things I've heard in a while. So how far do you reckon you've travelled?'

'Not got a clue. All I know is the lift chucked me around for about half an hour,' said George knowing that that was a slight exaggeration.

'So what are you going to do?'

'Haven't got a clue. I was kind of hoping you might be able to help me, or know someone that can.'

Peter shrugged. 'Not got a clue either. Unless...'

George held his breath.

'Well I can't really ask Mum and Dad if they'll help because they'll think I've lost the plot, but I suppose we could ask Molz if she's got any ideas. She loves things like this, she won't have any trouble believing you and you never know she might even know where Middlebridge is; if anyone will, she will.'

'OK. Who's Molz?

'My cousin, but don't you call her Molz, it'll wind her up. I just about manage to get away with it. You just call her Molly.'

'OK.'

'And if we can't find out where Middlebridge is then I suppose I could ask Mum and Dad if it's OK for you to stay over tonight, seeing as though you've got nowhere else to go.'

'Really would you do that?'

'Sure.'

'Thanks Peter, yeah, thanks a lot.' George felt his body unstiffen slightly. This was good.

'Oh, but George,' said Peter. 'Might be best when you meet them not to mention the lift and all that, if you know what I mean.'

George knew what he meant.

'Come on in then,' said Peter.

The inside of the house looked about ten times bigger than George had imagined it would be. It really was quite huge, and there were lots of people there. As he glanced around he noticed that some people looked to have pale green complexions. He was about to ask Peter why they looked green when Peter said. 'There she is.' He was pointing to a girl of similar age to them. She was wearing a worn orange dress, and was standing behind a small group of people, quietly listening in.

'Molz,' shouted Peter, to which all the people in the group turned around to catch her eavesdropping. She turned around and gave Peter the most serious of looks. 'You've made me look like a right one,' she said, walking towards them angrily. 'Now everyone'll think I was listening into their conversation.'

'Well you were,' said Peter laughing.

'No I wasn't, I was just listening to what Mrs Malloy had to say. Did you know that Mr Wangle thinks that he's found a Yuxy sanctuary at the end of his garden?'

'Molz,' said Peter, 'you really need to grow up and stop believing in all that kind of rubbish.'

'Who's this?'

'George.'

'Hello, I'm Molly.'

'Hiya Molly.' George thought that she was wearing way too much make-up, made her look real orange like. He imagined her scooping it out of the tub and slapping it on. She had shoulder length dark hair that was a bit on the dull side, and cloudy blue eyes.

'How do you know Peter then?' she asked.

'We've just met,' said Peter.

'Oh.'

'Listen Molz, do you know where Middlebridge is?'

'What's that?'

'A place.'

'Is it really? What a weird name.'

'So you don't know where it is then?'

Molly shook her head. 'No I don't. Why?'

'George is from there, and he's lost. He needs to get back.'

'Fancy someone of your age getting lost. How did you manage that?'

'Never mind that now,' said Peter turning to George. 'Plan B. Molz have you seen Mum and Dad? I need to see if he can stay over tonight.'

'But you don't even know him.'

'Long story, we'll tell you in a bit.'

'Oh OK.'

'Well have you seen them?'

'I saw Uncle James going into the kitchen about five minutes ago.'

'Come on then.'

George followed them into the kitchen.

Molly shook her head. 'You know Peter I can never get used to your house like this, it's just so confusing. I like it much better when it's smaller.'

George wondered what she was talking about.

'There he is,' said Peter.

A man with thick, greying hair and a slightly crooked nose was pouring a drink whilst leaning against the wall. He wore a badly fitting T-shirt tucked into some flannel trousers.

'Dad, this is George, he's a friend of mine,' said Peter.

'Hello there George, are you having a good time?'

'Oh-er-well,' began George, unsure of whether to tell the truth or not.

'Dad,' interrupted Peter. 'We just wondered since it's getting so late, and George has got such a long way to go home, would it be alright if he stayed over tonight?'

Mr Hubbins looked at George through heavy eyes. 'But it's Moderation Day tomorrow, are you sure your parents won't want you home with them tonight?' He rested a cumbersome hand on George's shoulder and took a swig of something violet.

'Well, er, no. I think it'll be OK.'

'Can I stay over as well?' asked Molly.

'Course you can. I'll phone your mum and dad and let them know,' said Mr Hubbins.

'Not bothered,' said Molly sulkily.

'I know you're not bothered Molly,' said Mr Hubbins. 'But I'll do it anyway. And George I should phone your parents too.'

'Er, well no, it'll be OK ...'

'They're at work,' said Peter quickly. 'We'll phone them in a bit.' Mr Hubbins tilted his head slightly, hesitated for a moment, then shrugged. 'Right then, oh and lights out by 11, is that clear?'

'*Yes Dad*,' said Peter. 'Well come on you two, we've got a lot to talk about.'

Peter's room was at the end of a short corridor, and was the untidiest room George had ever been in. The bed was hardly visible there was so much stuff on it. George wondered how anyone could sleep in a room like it. There were shelves all around that were crammed with all kinds of bottles and packets. George was dying to know what was in them all, but was still a bit too shy to ask.

'You sit here George, next to me,' said Molly, pushing a whole load of stuff off the bed. George sat down and felt something hard beneath him. He reached underneath and pulled out a small bottle – *Screaming Saccharin* – and placed it on the already overcrowded bedside cabinet.

Moments later they were talking about George's adventure, though George was suspicious as to whether deep down either of them, even Molly, truly believed him. But he just couldn't think of any way he could prove that he was from – well – from a different country – world – maybe even universe. It was all so ridiculous. But he was going to have to convince them one way or another because he really needed their help. He set about rooting through his pockets. He dug his hands deep into his Diesel jeans – surely there was something in there that would prove he was from somewhere else – he pulled out a five pound note and a bit of change. He emptied it all out onto the bed, and continued to rummage through his pockets.

'Look at this,' said Molly, much to George's surprise. 'What is it?'

'This? Money. Why? Don't you have money here?'

'No,' said Peter, examining it closely. 'What's it for? I've never seen anything like this before, have you Molz?'

'No, I haven't.'

George's eyes widened – maybe this was the way he could convince them all. 'Well, it's used to buy things.'

'What do you mean?'

'Just say I wanted some new clothes,' said George tugging at his Armani shirt. 'Well, I'd go to the shop, give them lots of this, and then they'd give me some new clothes.'

'But what's the point of that, wouldn't you just wish for them?' asked Molly flicking over a 20 pence piece.

'What do you mean?' said George. '*Wish* for them?'

'That's what we do,' said Molly.

'You mean, you can just wish for whatever you want – *and you get it?*'

'Yeah!' said Peter. 'Course.'

'No way! You're having me on.'

'No we're not, why would we do that?'

George was struggling to get his breath. '*Wow!* This is fantastic. I mean, imagine being able to make a wish and for it to come true, just like that. I'd have everything I ever wanted – the best clothes in the world – and a massive plasma screen in my bedroom – and hundreds, no thousands of computer games, and'

'George, stop!' said Molly laughing. 'It doesn't work like that. The whole wishing thing isn't that brilliant – honestly it isn't.'

'Yeah it is,' said Peter. 'But I think your way sounds much better than ours. Imagine being able to hand over pieces of metal and paper, and then being given whatever you want for it. Now that is amazing. I *so* want to go to your world.'

'It's a bit more complicated than that.'

George just couldn't understand why anyone would prefer his world to a world where wishes come true. 'Tell me about wishes and how you make them come true.'

'Well, ' said Molly. 'You can wish for anything you want, but every wish comes at a price.'

'Aw what? You mean you do have to pay for things after all?' sighed George.

'Not with this money thing, no,' said Molly. 'We can wish for whatever we want, so long as we're not too greedy.'

'Why, what happens if you're greedy?'

'If you wish for too many things, you have to suffer consequences. Really bad consequences,' said Molly.

'Like what?'

Molly looked a bit like she was going to cry. 'You get an illness, a disease called greening. The greedier you are the worse the disease gets – it can kill you in the end.'

'First your eyes go green,' said Peter. 'Then your skin gets greener and greener. You lose loads of weight and your hair and teeth start to fall out. In the end blood spurts out of your mouth so fast it kills you.'

'Aw what? That's gross!'

'Not so keen now?' asked Molly.

'Never said that. How long does it take to kill you?'

'That's the spirit George,' said Peter, slapping him a bit too hard on the back. 'You see I reckon I can have a lot of fun wishing, and still live to be about 45. And that's ancient.'

'Peter, it's not clever though is it? You're always over doing it. You'll regret it one day. I mean look at that lad from Leesome Falls - Anthony Lewis – he was only ten when he died from overwishing. If that's not enough to put you off then nothing is.'

'There might have been something else up with him as well,' argued Peter.

'You know it was overwishing that killed him. Even Sir Augustine had to admit it was, remember it was on the front page of *The Prying Post*.'

'Who's Sir Augustine?' asked George.

'He owns the E. House – biggest star in Leesome Shrouds!' said Peter. 'My hero.'

'The E. House, what's that?'

'The Enchantment Warehouse,' said Peter fondly. 'But we all call it the E. House. It's a massive warehouse with all sorts of great stuff in it. It's my favourite place ever. See all of this.' He pointed to everything in his room. 'I got it all from there. I go there every Saturday night with my mates, it's just fantastic.'

'Yeah, they all use up loads of wishes getting a right load of garbage,' said Molly. 'And then on Sunday they're all sick from overwishing. Sounds like great fun.'

'It is,' said Peter, 'I'd go there every night if Mum and Dad would let me, but they only let me go once a week. When I leave home I'm going to go there every night. George, don't let Molly scare you off wishing, it's not that bad, honestly, so long as you don't go too mad with it.'

Molly shook her head. 'It's not funny, don't encourage him.'

'I'm not – well not really,' said Peter grinning again. 'It's up to him if he chooses to overwish, isn't it? No one can make him do it can they?'

Molly didn't answer.

'Tell you what, George, if you're still here Saturday I'll take you with me to the E. House so you can see for yourself.'

'Oh, OK.' George really hoped that he wasn't going to be stuck here that long. Then he had a sudden thought; his heart definitely missed a beat. 'If wishes come true like you said they do, why don't I just wish to go back home? I don't know why I didn't think of it before.'

Peter shook his head. 'Sorry George, nice idea but it won't work. Transportation wish, not possible. The wish thing's complicated. I'm in my second year of Wishnomics and I still don't understand the half of it.'

George felt the disappointment crawl right through him. 'Oh, right. I'll just have to think of another way back then.'

'Course, and we will,' said Peter 'But first, tell us all about your world – and how much of this paper and metal you use.'

~

Bedtime came. George stood alone in the bedroom he'd been given. It was a plain room, unwelcoming almost, just an old bed, matching bedside cabinet, a clock and a brass lamp. He thought about his room at home, his TV, the soft bed, the curtains that were too long and his desk, piled high with homework. He was missing it all.

He walked over to the bed, sat down and closed his eyes. He could still feel his body shaking slightly. He sighed. This was definitely one of the worst days of his life. Not quite as bad as Mum leaving, but not far off. Now there was a possibility he might lose Dad too. What was he going to do if he was stuck here? He'd be all alone, miles from anyone he knew, and practically an orphan. But hang on, hadn't that been what he'd wanted so many times in his life. To just run away, to run and never stop running. Leave his dad that didn't care, his dad that didn't look after him, and his dad that didn't stop that Stuart Crocker and his gang from bullying him every day. That bullying that had ruined his life for six long years. George's thoughts went back to *that* afternoon, the day it had all started. He'd been walking home from school through the park when they'd approached him, and before he knew it they'd pinned him down to the ground. The memory of it was still so shocking George's body began to shake harder. He could still see those disgusting faces jeering down at him. He recalled the cruel laughter getting louder the more he struggled, and that embarrassing feeling of helplessness overcoming him. He'd been seriously outsized and outnumbered.

Stuart was trying to force George to admit to something. Trying to make him say that his dad was a murderer, that he'd buried his mum in the garden, and that all the rumours were true. But George couldn't say it – wouldn't say it – and never would say it, even though he had occasionally thought that perhaps it might be true. And when he had refused to say it Stuart had pushed handfuls of soil into his mouth, worms and all. The dirt clenched the moisture from his mouth and grated the back of his throat. George had seriously thought he was going to choke to death, to die there right on that spot. He remembered the feeling of his body go limp, his eyes slowly close, and his mind fade into death.

George shuddered, shook his head. He should try to go to sleep, forget about it. But then the nightmares would probably come. There just never was a way of escaping the vivid memories, and the fear they brought with them. Daylight, nighttime, it was all the same. No let up. That's why he'd had those thoughts sometimes. Those terrible thoughts, those of *wanting to end it all*, and the many ways he thought he could do it.

George gasped! He rubbed his head hard with both his hands. Gasped again. The air was too thin here. He got up off the bed, and quietly paced around the room until he felt calmer. Now he should definitely try to go to sleep before he let that Stuart into his head again. He pulled back the duvet, and crawled in. The sheets were cold and clammy against his skin.

He looked at his watch; Middlebridge time, teatime there, probably nearly midnight here. George wondered whether his dad had even realised that he was missing yet, if he hadn't realised by now then he would definitely realise in a couple of hours. But he wouldn't care anyway. Would anyone care? Course, the teachers at school tomorrow would wonder where he was, and he supposed Onion and Big Toe would miss him. And what would happen to Dad if he didn't get back for a week or two, everyone would be saying that he'd murdered his son too. He knew Dad would really struggle to cope. Then there'd probably be a visit – from the police. And he knew that if his dad couldn't answer their questions satisfactorily then, this time, George was sure, that they would lock him up.

But maybe his dad deserved it. NO, of course he didn't. George shook his head, what was he thinking, there was no way it was true, absolutely no way. He couldn't think like that. And of course Dad would miss him, deep down he really believed that... *didn't he*? So what he needed to do now was focus on a way to get back, so Dad wouldn't get into trouble. But how was he going to do that? It was seriously looking like he might be stuck here for two weeks – in Leesome Shrouds, the place name that sent shivers right through him.

But then on the positive side, two whole weeks in a place where wishes come true – he supposed it could be much worse, and this family had been really kind to him so far. He wondered what was going to happen next.

George yawned, and closed his eyes; maybe he *was* quite tired after all. Maybe the journey had tired him out; perhaps he had a bit of lift lag. He tucked himself up into a tight ball and for a while his mind drifted off back to the lift. He began to wonder about the parcel and how come it was addressed to him, and how come so many things that day had seemed so familiar.

-Chapter Three-

MODERATION DAY

George woke up with a jolt. He clenched his forehead with his hand and groaned. His eyes darted around the strangeness of the room. *No, No, No, No, No!* This couldn't be happening. Not to him. He was just ordinary – this sort of thing happened to, well, other people.

'Come on,' he hissed as he pulled at his hair and shook his head. 'Wake up!'

Slowly he let go of his hair and raised his head. He opened his watery eyes.

'Not a dream,' he muttered. 'But it must be – it has to be.'

He put his head back in his hands to help him think. A sudden thought of his dad rushed into his head. Oh no, he was going to kill him when he got home. He would. He'd say it was all his own fault, for getting into the stupid lift in the first place. He needed to find a way home, soon, before things got really serious.

George raised himself off the bed and walked over to the tapered window. It was becoming light outside and the houses opposite were glowing a curious orange. He leaned against the window ledge and stared out onto the unfamiliar street. For quite some time he stayed there wondering about the possibilities – the possibilities of wishing – of getting help – of finding a way home.

Disturbed by creaking floorboards outside the door, George tiptoed over to the door. He pressed his ear up against it. He could hear voices, and a commotion coming from down the hall.

A woman's voice, stern and loud. 'Peter, this really is the final straw, and on Moderation Day of all days!'

Peter's voice. 'Sorry Mum.'

'You should be, and you will be, wait till your father hears about this.'

'But it's not really my fault, it's...'

And the voices faded downstairs.

What time was it? He looked at his watch, 2.38am, in Middlebridge, seven hours later here. He wondered what to do. Should he go downstairs? No too soon, he would wait a while, until the arguing stopped.

George sat on the edge of the bed and thought about the last time *his* mum had shouted at him like that. Their final row he remembered it like it was yesterday.

He'd been playing out with Onion and Big Toe, or Simon and Tony, as they were known back then. They hadn't given each other nicknames until they were ten and about to go to high school. At this point they were only six. He was supposed to be home by seven o'clock but he'd been having such a great time making a tree-house that he'd completely lost track of time. It was only when it began to get dark that he thought to check the time. George recalled that jolt in his chest when he looked down at his watch – *8.30*. He was going to be in big trouble: no not just big trouble, *massive*. There was no way he could go home. Ten minutes later George found himself alone in the woods, crouched up in the tree-house, jacket wrapped around his knees for warmth. By 11 o'clock the woods were black, groaning and chilling to the core. Time to go home.

George smiled sadly as he remembered himself standing at the front door, trembling with the cold and an awesome fear – the bravery it took for him to knock. The look on Mum's tear sodden face, the shouting, the hugging, then the shouting and hugging again. That night he'd slept in Mum and Dad's bed, Mum's arms wrapped tightly around him all night.

George curled up on the bed and closed his eyes, trying to remember how safe he had felt that night and how he had wanted to stay like that forever, just there in her arms. A tear dropped down onto the pillow. He closed his eyes tighter. And slowly he dozed off.

George jumped. Footsteps coming up the stairs and a voice. 'George, George are you awake?' Molly's voice. He sat up, rigid on the bed holding his breath. 'Breakfast's ready, come down when you want. See you in a bit then.'

George listened to the sound of her fading footsteps. He should just go downstairs now, he was going to have to do it some time, so might as well do it now, get it out of the way. Shaking inside he walked out onto the creaking floor, down the hall, then the stairs and into the main living area. Molly and Mr Hubbins were sitting at the table having breakfast.

'Good morning George,' said Mr Hubbins raising himself very slowly and carefully off the chair. 'Happy Moderation Day, come, sit, have some breakfast with us.'

George looked around the room. It was way smaller than it had been the night before, way, way smaller. There was an old bookcase in the corner, a table with six chairs, and a maroon, velvet sofa, all crammed into the tiny room. He sat down at the table next to Mr Hubbins, Molly was sitting opposite staring at him, and stuffing something that resembled a blue banana into her mouth.

A noise at the front door, George turned around to see what it was. A woman with shoulder length brown hair came through the door. Her blue eyes were flaming red and aggravated. Peter followed quickly behind her, shuffling his feet, head down, the tips of his ears bright red.

Mr Hubbins went over. 'I got your note, what was it this time?'

She shook her head. 'Peter had something stuck on his forehead, hospital job, we had to have it removed.' There was a tone of disgust in her voice. She took off her coat and went to hang it on a hook behind the door.

'What was it?' asked Mr Hubbins.

'I'd rather not say in front of the children.'

'Oh, I see.' Mr Hubbins pursed his lips and shook his head. 'It's your own fault Peter. If *you'd* stop wishing things on people they'd stop wishing things on you. Honestly, haven't you learnt that yet?'

Peter raised his head in defence. George could see a patch of stitches on his forehead. 'I know who did this, and there's no way I deserved it. This was way out of order.'

'Who was it?' asked Molly.

'That Brian Bones again,' said Peter.

Mr Hubbins shook his head. 'And precisely *why* did he do it?'

'Because I gave him some Swearing Syrup yesterday, that's all. I'm going to get him back for this,' said Peter frowning – then wincing. 'I swear I am.'

'Mrs Hubbins turned around and walked towards the table. 'Peter, I've told you time and again, leave it. He'll only get you back again, and who knows he could wish for something worse on you the next time. Though what could be worse than *that* I don't know. I'm going to have a word with his mother about this.'

'Don't Mum, I can handle it! Anyway he'll just deny it.'

Mrs Hubbins' eyes flashed at George. She walked over to Molly and kissed her on the top of her head. 'Anyway enough about that for now, we'll sort your punishment out later, I see we have a guest.'

'Yeah,' said Molly. 'This is George. He's our new friend.'

'Well hello George,' said Mrs Hubbins smiling warmly. 'Sorry you've come into our home under such unfortunate circumstances, things aren't usually like this around here.'

Molly stifled a snigger that suggested to George that they were, and from what he already knew about Peter it didn't surprise him one bit.

Just then George saw something out of the corner of his eye, something pale blue that was moving across the floor. He turned around. It was something cat sized, furry, a bit like a cuddly toy. It walked over to an empty bowl, sat down, turned around to look at them all and growled softly exposing a nasty set of jagged teeth.

Mrs Hubbins shook her head. 'Has no one fed Alan yet? Honestly...' She reached up into a cupboard and pulled out a tin: *Barbed Wire Chunks in Gravy*.

'What's that?' yelled George without thinking.

'What do you mean what's that?' asked Mr Hubbins in surprise.

Oh Oh, he'd put his foot in it. How was he going to explain this?

Mr Hubbins eyed George suspiciously. 'How come you don't know what a dinky is?'

George said nothing. He looked over at Peter. He was laughing as widely as his stitches would allow.

Mr Hubbins shook his head. 'I thought there was something odd going on when you said your parents wouldn't mind you staying over on Moderation Eve. Now what's going on?'

'Well,' said Peter. 'You might as well tell them the truth. I mean you're going to have to tell them at some time.'

'What?' George wasn't prepared.

'Tell them about Middlebridge, and that lift that brought you here,' said Peter raising his eyebrows.

'Be quiet Peter. Don't be ridiculous,' said Mr Hubbins, giving him a friendly dig in the ribs. George squirmed down into the seat. He knew that they were going to think he was mad.

Then Molly joined in. 'You are going to have to tell them at some point, you've got nowhere to stay. And anyway, they might be able to help.'

'Look, what is this?' said Mr Hubbins, a bemused look on his face. 'What's going on?'

'Just tell them George,' said Molly. 'It'll be OK, honestly.'

George stammered and stuttered as he began to tell them about his journey. When he had finished, Mr and Mrs Hubbins sat in silence.

'More tea anyone?' asked Mr Hubbins, offering around an old blue china teapot, all the while staring at George.

'Well,' said Mrs Hubbins sympathetically. 'I suppose you could be telling the truth, I mean, I have heard of this kind of thing before. I remember a woman I once worked with saying that she believed in this kind of thing, but to be honest with you I just thought she was barking mad.'

Peter laughed loudly, and clutched his forehead. 'Ouch!'

Molly nodded her head. 'We thought George was too, until we listened to what he had to say. George's world doesn't have wishes that come true.'

'No?' said Mr Hubbins. 'How weird is that. How does that work then?'

'Show them those metal things George,' said Molly.

George showed Mr and Mrs Hubbins the money, and the lift timetable, and began to tell them about Middlebridge, and England. It took a while before Mr and Mrs Hubbins looked like they were taking him seriously, but eventually Mrs Hubbins gave a sign that she was definitely starting to believe him. 'Oh dear your parents are going to be worried sick,' she said.

'Well, my dad will be,' said George, 'I er – I don't have a mum.'

'Oh,' replied Mrs Hubbins, awkwardly bowing her head. 'Well we must do all we can to get you back to your dad then.'

Molly jumped up. 'Maybe we should take George back to the Banishing Block, see if there's any sign of the lift today.'

'That's as good a starting point as any I suppose,' said Mrs Hubbins. 'You could all have quite an adventure couldn't you? But now Peter, listen to me carefully, I'm warning you, don't you *dare* get into that lift if it's there, or there'll be trouble. I mean it, *real trouble*! I know what you're like. Promise.'

Peter shook his head. 'I won't, honestly.' His hands were placed firmly behind his back, George suspected that he was crossing his fingers.

Mrs Hubbins glanced at her watch. 'Goodness me, would you look at the time, that visit to the hospital's put us right back. We've only a couple of hours before Edwin Brown and his family arrive for Moderation Day dinner and we're nowhere near ready. Come on everyone let's get tidied up.'

'But what about the Banishing Block?' said Molly.

'As soon as the house is ready you can go and have a quick look,' said Mrs Hubbins. 'And I mean quick, you must be back for dinner, do you hear me?'

'OK then,' said Peter jumping up. 'But let's hurry.'

Mrs Hubbins laid a soft hand on George's shoulder. 'George, there isn't much you can do to help, but there are some books over there in the corner if you want to occupy yourself for a while. You might find some of them quite interesting.'

They all set about their chores and George settled into reading a story called *Alvin of Green Gables.*'

After a while George went to put it back on the shelf, it was boring him. Peter was nearby checking his forehead out in a mirror.

'Is it sore?' asked George.

'Nah, it'll be like new by tomorrow anyway. *Stitch in time saves Nine Cream* you know.'

George just nodded. 'Ah right.' This place was definitely weird.

'And here,' said Peter. 'Never mind reading that, have a look at this. He picked up a colossal book called *Guidelines for Greening* and dropped it onto George's lap. 'They reckon to stay healthy you shouldn't use any more than ten wishes a day, but just say you really want something and you need to know how sick it's going to make you, then this is the book you need.'

This was definitely more George's kind of thing. 'Thanks.'

'No probs. Best get on though, before Mum gets on at me. Tell you what, I'm glad you're here or it would have been much worse earlier on.' Peter walked away.

George opened the book on page five. There were dozens of pictures of really naff pullovers, available between eight and ten wishes, with minimum sickness. There was no way George would be seen dead in any of them. The further on into the book he went the more wishes things cost. On the very back page there were photos of a house that required 72,000 wishes. It had 18 bedrooms, 16 bathrooms, and indoor and outdoor swimming pools. The garden stretched out to the sea, where there was a fabulous yacht. George loved it, he could live there, he knew he could. He looked to see what the consequences would be for a house like that:

MEDICAL ADVICE
Moderate sickness daily for 15 years.
Severe sickness occurs at 20 years.
Life expectancy – 25 years.

George shuddered. To think if he wished for such a thing now, he would be dead by the time he was 38. Maybe Molly was right not to get so excited about this wish thing after all.

Perhaps he would postpone his secretly planned afternoon of wishing for just a bit longer.

A sudden slap on the arm brought George back to reality.

Molly was there. 'Come on George. We're all done. Let's go and look for that lift.'

The Banishing Block seemed further away than George had remembered. He must have been in a daze for most of the journey yesterday.

'What's this Moderation Day about anyway?' asked George.

Peter grinned. 'It's the day we're supposed to moderate our wishes, but we don't, we all end up doing the opposite. Well I do anyway, Molz here doesn't. It's great because it's the only day of the year Mum and Dad don't lecture me about overwishing.'

'Just around the corner now,' said Molly.

George could feel his head beginning to hurt, reeling with the hellish recollections from the previous day. They turned the corner, George took a step back. There it was! Hideous, dark, cold, forbidding. He watched Peter and Molly run over. Molly was the first to get there. 'No sign of anything here.' She was examining the stones. 'No sign of anything here at all.'

George walked over, and stared at the exact place the lift had been. 'It's like I said, it just disappeared.' He knocked hard on the stones.

'Is that how you cut your hands?'

'Yeah.'

Peter gasped. 'Hey listen, I've got an idea. Why don't you just wish for the lift to come to you? You never know it might work.'

'He can't do that!'

'Why not, you got any better ideas?'

'It's too dangerous!'

'Why?' asked George. 'I think it's a great idea. It's so obvious.'

'George you can't. Think about it. You might not have any control over the lift when it leaves Leesome Shrouds. What if you get in it and the only place it stops is Helcrix. It's much too dangerous, honestly, don't listen to Peter, he's always full of bad ideas.'

'Maybe Molz is right. Maybe we shouldn't be looking for the lift at all. You could end up anywhere. At least with that timetable you know for sure that it's stopping at Middlebridge. I mean none of us has got a clue what all those other places are like. They could be worse than Helcrix for all we know. I mean that Domain of Morgue place sounds a bit scary.'

George thought that Leesome Shrouds didn't sound too great either. But he was inclined to agree with Molly that it could be dangerous. It was beginning to look like he might be stuck here for the full two weeks.

A bus hissed as it pulled up at George's side, he felt his face whiten. This was the last thing he had wanted to see, had expected to see. 'OH NO!' he said quietly.

'What?' asked Molly.

George couldn't move. 'There's someone I know on that bus.'

-Chapter Four-

STUART

'Who?'

'That lad, the one with the black hair. He's from Middlebridge.'

George wondered if he should go after the bus – no way! *But it might be his only chance.* He had to. He ran after the bus, but the driver carried on accelerating up the road, ignoring him completely. George stared after it. Stuart Crocker, the person he hated most in the world was here in Leesome Shrouds, and he might be the only person who could help him. A movement on the back seat. Stuart turned around, looked straight at George, smirked, or snarled, George couldn't tell which, and then the bus was gone.

He ran back to the others. 'It's definitely Stuart Crocker, I'd recognise him anywhere.'

'Maybe it was just someone that looks like him,' said Molly. 'I mean, they say we all have a double don't they?'

'No, it was definitely him, I swear. I've seen him up close often enough.' George didn't want to mention the bullying. 'I need to speak to him, he might know another way home. Where does that bus go?'

'The E. House,' said Peter grinning.

'How far is it?'

'We could be there in less than ten minutes.'

'Will you show me the way?'

'Course we will,' said Peter. 'Fantastic. Come on then, what are we waiting for?'

Molly shook her head. 'We shouldn't really, we said we wouldn't be too long. And Peter, what if you use up too many wishes in there today, your mum and dad will go mad.'

Peter just shrugged. 'No they won't. It's Moderation Day. They'll be sorted. Anyway who's going to tell them? Look I'll take it easy, honestly, still feeling a bit rough from Saturday.'

'That's what I mean, it was only two days ago you were in there,' said Molly. 'And there's no way you'll take it easy, you say that every time, but you never do. Bet you two wishes, you end up using more than twenty wishes in there today.'

'You're on, Molz,' said Peter. They shook on it.

They arrived at the E. House. It was weird, but George could swear that a sort of *enchanted* feeling swept right through him. He looked up at the glass skyscraper. Thousands of brightly coloured boxes and bottles crammed the windows as if wanting to burst out. Inside there were bright posters everywhere and lots of posters of a man on them – the same man.

George asked. 'Who's that?' The man was smiling a broad smile but a curl at the edges of his mouth and a narrowing in his blue eyes made him look, well – evil, or so George thought.

'Sir Augustine,' said Peter proudly. 'It's because of him we've got all this.'

George had to admit it *was* pretty amazing. Perhaps he was wrong.

'What's the plan then?' asked Molly.

'Let's just meet up in an hour,' said Peter.

Molly sighed. 'Peter! We need to help George find this Stuart, you can't just go off and leave like that.'

'It's OK Molly,' said George quickly. He didn't want his new friends to find out that he was being bullied; it made him feel ashamed. 'I'd rather look for Stuart on my own. Anyway you don't know what he looks like, so it'll be quicker this way.'

'You sure?' she said.

'Yeah.'

'Well I suppose I do need to do a bit of shopping, need to get some anti-greening eye drops, that sort of thing.'

George wondered why Molly needed anti-greening eye drops. Maybe her mum and dad were sick.

'OK,' said Peter. 'Back here in an hour then?'

Molly headed off towards the make-up department.

'Before I go George, a word of advice,' said Peter. 'If you decide to get anything, make sure it's not more than about 25 wishes, or you'll be sick as a Beazlefriar tomorrow. Last year, like an idiot I stupidly used up 43, I'll never do that again. See it's easy to get carried away in here, there are so many fantastic things. Like this.' He picked up a purple bottle. 'Look – *Forgetful Potion*. And you only have to use two wishes to get it. But you get six doses – that's six lots of fun for just two wishes. Bargain. Don't know how they do it.'

'But what's it for?'

'Use your imagination George, that's what you have to do in here.'

'But why would *you* want to be forgetful?'

'Not me you moron, I'd give it to someone else. Like a dose to Mum and Dad late one Sunday night. It says here that one dose lasts 12 hours, right? So then they'd forget to wake me up for school on Monday morning. Now do you see what I mean? Look, I'm going to head off now, I saw something on the way in that I really want to get for Molz and there's not many left – it's just perfect. Tell you what, I'm going to have some fun with this.' And he walked away laughing.

George decided to start his search on the top floor and work his way down. On the eighth floor he had become distracted by the menu board in the cafe.

```
                        MENU
                       Starters
                    Bunion onions
                         ....
                     Main Course
   Polyp and mushroom pie, served with a corn on the cob
                  and a bone meal gravy
                       Dessert
   Cellulite jelly served with a warm pimple custard

                         ....

        Cheshire Set cheese with You're crackers.

   All meats and cheeses are from free-range humans.
```

George gagged. He was seriously hoping that he hadn't eaten anything like that at breakfast earlier, though he had to admit the food had tasted seriously good, particularly that fleshy nut shaped thing he'd eaten. Just then George felt something dig him hard on the shoulder. He turned round. Stuart was there, just staring at him. He felt his blood singe his face.

Stuart was everything everyone wanted to be at school. Tall, black hair, tanned, perfect teeth, shiny blue eyes, muscles, tough. He always wore the best clothes and the smartest trainers, and he fancied himself lots, but then so did all the girls. And his family just so happened to be the richest in Middlebridge.

'Well if it isn't the murderer's son,' said Stuart folding his arms, smiling smugly.

George felt the hatred for him seethe inside. Hatred for him and all his friends, all of them that had made his life so difficult, sometimes almost impossible, over the years. But now he needed his help, so he told himself to try to be nice, at least for as long as he could be.

'It's not true, my dad would never have done that,' said George quietly.

Stuart pushed him on the top of his arm. 'Then where is she, pretty boy? Ran off with the milkman did she?'

George said nothing. He couldn't say anything, he had no answers. And what was that with the pretty boy?

Stuart leered at him. 'So you're an Interglobal Traveller?'

'I don't know, what's that?'

'Oh! I get it! Georgee boy's parents haven't told you about this have they? Not that your mum could anyway because she's probably buried ten foot deep in your cellar.'

George could feel his whole body shaking... but he had to stay calm. 'We don't have a cellar,' he whispered.

Stuart laughed.

Just get some answers, and get away from this. 'So what have my parents got to do with this?'

'They must have known that you'd be able to travel to different Globes, they must have just decided not to tell you. Wonder why?'

George shrugged.

'How did you get here then Georgee boy? Down the toilet?'

'I just got into a lift at Middlebridge train station, and ended up here.'

Stuart raised one eyebrow, seemed interested. 'That's your mode of transport is it? A lift eh? Dead easy.'

'Well it wasn't.'

'Oogh, mummy's boy. Oops, sorry I almost forgot, no mummy any more.'

'George just wanted to turn and run, but knew that would be a mistake at this point. 'Look, I just really need to get back home to my dad, he'll be going out of his mind.'

'Doubt it, he probably won't even notice you're gone. And anyway he's probably glad you're not at home – given him a bit of time to spend with your mum's corpse.'

George felt his whole body tense, his fists were packed so tight he could feel his nails piercing the skin on the palms of his hands. *But still he needed answers, he couldn't lose his cool, not now.* 'So is the lift my only way back?' He realised his voice was shaking, he hoped Stuart wouldn't notice.

'Why should I tell you anything, you piece of crap?'

Time for a change of tactics. 'Well because you know so much about everything.' He felt sick about what he was about to say. 'Everyone at school's always saying how smart you are, and now I see why.'

Stuart looked impressed, puffed his chest out. 'Yeah?'

'Yeah definitely. I bet you know everything there is to know about all of this don't you?'

'Pretty much.'

'Bet you'd even be able to tell me how I'd be able to get back.'

'Course I do. Go to your lift the day the clocks change, in two weeks' time.'

'That's the only way?'

'Yeah, you're well and truly stuck here till then.'

George felt dizzy – two weeks. 'Right!'

'Hey, don't look so upset, make the most of it, I mean Leesome Shrouds is an awesome place to be stuck in, don't you think?'

'Suppose.'

'No suppose about it.'

'When you said my parents haven't told me, what did you mean?'

'Well at least one of them must know that you can travel Interglobally, because one of them will be able to do it too. They'll have travelled in exactly the same way you did.'

'You really do know loads of stuff don't you?'

Stuart tilted his head smartly to the side.

'So either my mum or dad will have been able to use the lift?'

'Yeah. It's a family thing you see. I get it from my dad's side. We've used the mines for hundreds of years, that's our families way of getting around. It'll be the same in your family, you'll be the only family that can use that lift. I met a girl once who has to travel through sewage pipes to get around. Imagine that? Disgusting or what?'

'Don't think I'd bother.'

'Bet you would,' said Stuart. 'When you hear this...'

George said nothing.

'Do you know how you can wish for whatever you want in Leesome Shrouds?'

'Yeah – so?'

'Well how great is that?'

'Great if you don't mind being sick.'

'I can't believe I'm going to be the one to tell you this, this is the most fantastic part of the whole thing,' said Stuart, a greedy smile spreading across his face. 'You're not going to believe this but...*you* won't be affected by overwishing.'

'What? You mean that I can wish for whatever I like – without ever getting sick?'

'That's exactly what I mean. I just love it here – I've got everything I ever wanted.'

George said nothing, but felt a wave of excitement swell throughout his body. Was this true? Stuart's eyes darted over to a woman in an official uniform. 'Oh oh! I have to go! See you back at school. Oh and don't think anything's changed, you're still going to get a good kicking when you're back in Middlebridge.'

Not so brave when you've not got your gang with you though are you? In fact you've been kind of helpful – for you anyway. George watched Stuart's dark head disappearing into the crowd. 'But wait, I have more questions...'

But Stuart was well and truly gone.

George slumped down onto a nearby sofa, thoughts whooshing around in his head. Wouldn't his dad have told him about all of this, if he'd known about it? But then, maybe it was his mum that knew, maybe she was the one that had been the Global Traveller. What if she'd taken him to see the lift before, when he was younger? It did look familiar. And the smell on the parcel – roses – was it her perfume? It could have been, he couldn't remember. But surely his dad would have told him if he'd known. He had always said that honesty was important, which meant he'd always been honest about everything, didn't it?

George heaved himself up, thoughts rampaging through his brain. Maybe it was Stuart that was the one that was lying, but why would he? He had nothing to gain from doing that did he, but then he really did hate George, and had been tormenting him for the last six years, maybe he was doing that now, just tormenting him that bit more.

Then George had an idea. He could overwish today, and see if he was sick in the morning. See if that Stuart was telling him the truth. Yes, that's what he'd do.

George peered at his watch. He had ten minutes left until he was due to meet Molly and Peter. He quickly grabbed a shopping basket. He didn't much feel like shopping, but he needed to know the truth.

The first item he was tempted with was *New Skin Potion.* Inside the small bottle was a liquid that looked like melted-down skin.

All for just three wishes! Just think, no more spots. He threw a handful into his basket, and carried on with his shopping spree.

Soon it was time to head back to the meeting place. Molly was waiting for him. She peered into his basket. In the short time he had been shopping he had found lots of things he wanted. Alongside the *New Skin Potion* were three packets of *Perfect Hair Powder*, two bottles of *Ice White Tooth Enamel*, and a *Flat Screen Crystal Ball* from the Foreseeable Future Department.

'George that's about 40odd wishes; take it from me you'll be really ill in the morning if you get that lot. You should put some back.'

'It's OK Molly,' said George. 'Don't worry about me I can handle it, I know what I'm doing.'

'No you don't George, honestly you don't. You've been listening to Peter too much.'

'No I haven't.'

'I've just seen him, and for someone who's not overwishing today he's not doing half bad. I reckon he's already used up about 23 wishes and he's not finished yet. Looks like I'm going to win that bet.'

'Yeah but he said he was getting something for you.'

Molly stopped dead, grabbed George's arm. '*Oh no*, he didn't did he?'

'Yeah.'

She shook her head. 'Oh no!'

'What's up?'

'I really don't like Peter's surprises.'

'Maybe it's something nice.'

'Trust me it isn't.' She resumed walking. 'So you didn't find Stuart then, or were you too busy shopping?'

'No,' lied George. He didn't feel he could tell her that perhaps he could wish for whatever he wanted without consequence. 'You were right, it must have just been someone that looked like him.'

'Well try not to worry too much. We'll find another way home for you, we will. Hey, the Tunnel of Trances is open the day after tomorrow, that might be just what you need.'

'What's the Tunnel of Trances?'

'It's where drealities happen,' said Molly, 'Well for 15 minutes anyway, and only once a week.'

'A dreality, never heard that word before, what does it mean?'

'When a dream becomes a reality. Whatever you want to happen to you most in the world will happen to you in there.'

'Well what I want most is to find a way home.'

'Well the Tunnel of Trances will show you the way then,' said Molly. 'One thing's for sure, whatever does happen to you in there, you'll remember it for the rest of your life.'

Maybe she was right, this could be the answer.

Molly grabbed his arm. 'Come on then, let's get going.'

George was reluctant to leave, but thought it for the best because if he used up any more wishes there was a possibility that he might be shockingly ill tomorrow, and wouldn't Stuart just love that!'

'We just have to hand in our wishes.'

'How do you mean?'

'They'll just take a thumb prick of blood, you won't feel a thing.'

George hesitated, looked into his basket. 'I'm not sure.'

'Don't be soft it doesn't hurt. Years ago they used to have to drain the wish serum straight from your heart, with a huge needle. Some people used to pass out with the pain.'

George handed his basket to the lady behind the counter, she shook her head. 'You're going to be seriously ill tomorrow, if you take all of these at once.'

'I think I'll be OK,' replied George smiling.

'You're grinning now,' she said. 'Tomorrow will be a very different story, mark my words young man.'

George flinched as she pricked his finger with a long needle. She shook her head, tutting all the while. When leaving the shop he heard her say to her colleague. 'I keep telling the boss that there should be an age limit in here, but will he listen? No! Seems to me all he's bothered about is doing good trade and being famous. I mean that poor lad's much too young to know any better, don't you think?'

~

Later that night, when George was in bed he was awakened by a commotion from down the corridor. He got out of bed and quietly made his way towards the door. He opened it slightly.

'It's really not funny! I've been up half the night with this,' whispered Molly very loudly. She was standing outside Peter's door.

Peter was laughing so hard he was doubled over, his legs crossed.

'I thought it was weird you making me a drink earlier on, I just can't believe I was stupid enough to drink it. And George warned me that you were buying me a present. How dumb am I? Now give me something to get rid of this.'

Peter shook his head, still laughing.

'*You'd* better have something for this Peter. Tell me you do?'

He wiped away the tears that were streaming down his face.

'*Peter* this isn't funny any more. Go into your room and get me something for this. I mean it! NOW!'

He shrugged his shoulders, and still laughing went into his room. A minute later he came out and handed her a small red bottle. Molly snatched it from him. She hobbled off towards the bathroom.

'What was it?' whispered George down the corridor.

'*Itchy Arse Powder*,' replied Peter, laughing again and closing the door behind him.

-Chapter Five-

THE WISHES

George couldn't sleep. He was waiting for the sickness to occur. Peter had said that he usually felt it at about three in the morning, starting with a stomach ache. George watched the clock tick to three, then to four. By five he was asleep again. He only awoke when he heard the floorboards in the hallway creaking again. Someone was making their way noisily down the stairs. He looked at the clock again, 10am, and still no sickness. It looked like Stuart had been telling him the truth. How amazing was that. He, ordinary George Price could wish for whatever he wanted. He should wish for some things now. No, not now, someone was up and about, they could come up and catch him. No, he'd do it tonight. He went to the door but didn't open it: there was a problem. Wasn't it going to look suspicious to Molly and Peter that he wasn't sick from all the overwishing he'd done at the E. House yesterday? How stupid was he? He should have thought about this before. Now he needed an excuse – a reason why he wasn't being sick. What was he going to do? George stared numbly at the clock for half an hour and he still hadn't thought of an excuse. Maybe he should just say it was beginner's luck, or maybe he could *wish* himself to be sick – no, too risky – he could end up in any state.

Then, a great idea! The sickness tablets! He went over to his jacket, unzipped his pocket and reached inside for the box of pills. He removed the instructions –

Dosage: One to four tablets daily.
One tablet – Slight queasiness.
Two tablets – Stomach cramps with occasional vomiting.
Three tablets – Headaches, and stomach cramps with regular vomiting.
Four tablets – Fever, headaches, and excruciating stomach cramps with continuous vomiting.

Side effects
Healthy complexion, sparkling eyes, shiny hair, strong nails, blemish free skin, superior hearing, improved brain capacity and function.

'Crazy!' He stared at the instructions for quite a while. Deciding how many to take was proving difficult. The thought of making himself sick was – well – sickening. He definitely wouldn't take four tablets, the sickness would be too severe, but then he did have to make his overwishing look convincing. Three, he would take three. He quickly put the sickly green pills into his mouth, and gulped them down with some water.

The instructions had said that the tablets would start to work after ten minutes. George fidgeted with his hands as he paced up and down the room. The minutes ticked by.

'Ow!' he said, as he clutched his head with both hands.

'Oogh!' he moaned, as his left hand reached down to his stomach.

'Two,' he groaned. 'I should've only taken two, what was I thinking?'

Now he was definitely ready to convince everyone that he was sick from overwishing.

As he walked into the living room his stomach made a noise like water going down a plughole.

Molly screwed her face up at him. 'Are you OK? Sounds like you've got it bad.'

Mrs Hubbins got up and put her arm around him. 'Oh dear,' she said shaking her head furiously. She led him over to a nearby chair. 'Has that wonderful son of mine being leading you astray? I'm going to have words with him about this. He's always doing this, encouraging people to overwish, and that's three times he's been to that blasted Enchantment Warehouse this week, thinks his father and I haven't noticed, thinks just because it was Moderation Day yesterday that it's OK. Well it's not, wait till he gets down here.'

'It's not Peter's fault, honestly,' said George, 'I just couldn't help it, there were so many fantastic things there. Everyone did warn me about this, even Peter.'

'Did they dear?' said Mrs Hubbins, the redness in her face turning to a mild shade of pink. 'Well listen to me, George, you'll soon learn that greed only brings sickness and unhappiness to yourself. The sooner you grasp that fact, the more contented you'll be whilst you're in Leesome Shrouds. And another thing George – you have to try to find a way back to your dad and you're not going to be in any fit state to do that if you're overwishing all the time now are you?'

George knew she was right. 'No. But I'll be better for the Tunnel of Trances tomorrow. I will.'

'OK dear,' she said rubbing him on his back, causing him to retch. 'Enough of the lecturing.'

'George we're just off to *The Wisherman's Rest* for lunch,' said Molly, now strangely unaware of George's predicament. 'You can come too if you want?'

'No – I – er – I don't think I could stomach it.' He clutched his hands to his stomach. 'Ooogh.'

'George, are you sure you're going to be alright? asked Mrs Hubbins. 'We can stay here with you if you want.'

'No, no, it's OK. I think I might have to go back to bed for a bit though.'

'Good idea,' said Mrs Hubbins. 'Looks like you need to. We probably won't be back until about three o'clock so if you need anything while we're gone just knock on the door next to Peter's room, and wake up that good for nothing husband of mine.'

'OK, thanks.'

'We'll be off then.'

As Molly was going out of the door he heard her say. 'I'm going to have the puree of eyeball soup.' The mere mention of the word *eyeball* had George's stomach doing somersaults. He staggered up to his room. He had already decided that he would wish himself back to normal. Sitting down on the edge of the bed he made his wish. He waited for the sickness to leave, and he waited. And waited.

The vomiting only began to subside around the time he heard Molly and Mrs Hubbins coming home. Perhaps he should go down now, he wasn't feeling too bad.

Then! A sudden realisation swept over him, causing him to shudder slightly – *he could wish for whatever he wanted without being sick.* He had completely forgotten, because he had been too busy being sick. He sat up straight, smiled, and decided there and then that he wouldn't go down at all today – he would stay in his room and do some wishing. He was feeling much, much better now.

He was going to start right away – with that Rolex watch he had always wanted – the one with the blue face and the platinum strap. He had a picture of it in his desk drawer at home, one that he'd ripped out of a magazine, somehow he'd always known that he would get one – one day. He sat at the edge of the bed and took in an excited breath. Removed his old watch and threw it down onto the bedside cabinet. He closed his eyes and held out his arm. He was about to make his first ever proper wish. He took in a very deep breath, and made the wish with all his heart, like Peter had told him he would need to do. He felt something cold and heavy against his wrist. He couldn't look. Did he really have a Rolex? Very slowly he opened his eyes – wide. And there it was. A million times better than any picture. He stared at it for at least ten minutes, feeling distractedly happier than he had since he had stepped into the lift. But that wasn't all he wanted. Oh no, there was so much more to wish for.

All that afternoon, and into the evening George wished, and wished, and wished some more, until his wishes began to knock the plaster off the walls and the room began to bulge. But he was sure he could fit a few more things in, especially in that far corner. But what else did he need – or more to the point what else did he want?

The one wish that couldn't come true – to go home.

-Chapter Six-

THE TUNNEL OF TRANCES

The morning of the Tunnel of Trances arrived, George waited up in his room until he heard the others go downstairs. He fought his way to the door and opened it. Several boxes spilled out into the hallway. He really had overdone it. He wondered if he could *wish* any of them back. After all he didn't really need that rowing machine, did he? He shoved the boxes back up onto the pile and forced his way back into the room. He picked up the nearest box – there was a receipt inside.

REFUND POLICY

Refunds are guaranteed for up to eight hours*

If you wish to extend the warranty of this guarantee please refer to 'Wishing Guidelines 2001'.

Items can be returned wish free, but must be in original condition and packaging.

*Refunds will not be granted from the moment sickness occurs.

George shrugged; he didn't understand, so in the end he decided that he would just have to keep it all. He went back out into the hallway, placed his shoulder against the door and pushed hard against it until he heard it click, then made his way downstairs. He was feeling incredibly nervous this morning; what if this Tunnel of Trances didn't show him the

way to get home, what would he do then? It really was his only hope.

Molly and Peter were waiting by the door for him.

Molly looked at him and smiled, 'You OK?'

'I'm fine,' said George. 'Feeling a lot better than I did yesterday.'

'Good,' she said. 'Come on then, let's go to the Tunnel of Trances.'

Half an hour later the three of them stopped in the middle of the road, on a street with high privets along both sides. Staring down at a metal cover inset into the road George sighed. 'Is that it, a grid?'

'You won't be saying that when you come out,' said Molly. 'Promise you that.'

George wasn't sure. Then he heard a noise. Grinding metal, like a metal handle being turned.

Peter rubbed his hands. 'It's opening up.'

George watched as the grid began to break up, shatter into a thousand pieces. He could hear them implode down into a black hole. There was a metal ladder dropping down into the darkness. Peter was first down, quickly followed by Molly. George stood at the edge, and stared into the hole.

'Hurry up,' said an impatient boy behind him. 'There's a whole load of people that'll go down before you if you're too chicken?'

George decided that he was quite keen to get down into the dark and dingy hole after all. He held a tight grip on the ladder and slowly descended into the abyss. Deeper and deeper he went, hearing only the sound of his own rapid breathing, and the squeaking of his trainers on the metal rungs. The air was warm, musty and uncomfortable. The smell of damp dirt soaked his nostrils, making him feel slightly sick. Pausing for a moment, he gasped for breath, and peered over his shoulder down into the blackness. Then he looked up – just a tiny pinprick of light. He shuddered. How far down did this hole go exactly? It was getting too hot down here. *Come on! Keep going – home – think of home.*

Several minutes later George's foot touched the ground.

'YES!'

He hastily un-clung himself from the ladder and wiped his sweating forehead on his sleeve. He turned around. There was nothing much to see but some flickering flames in a deep, dark tunnel. For several long minutes he carefully made his way along the noiseless passageway. The acrid smell of soil faded away. He could smell something else now, something he was sure he recognised. There was a door ahead, he rushed over, he knew this door well. There was a key in the lock, he turned it slowly, then opened the door and stepped in. The first thing he saw was the instantly recognisable wallpaper of his hallway at home. He was back in Middlebridge. He could hear voices and laughing coming from the kitchen. Realising that somehow he now had his school satchel on his shoulder, he slid it down his arm and dumped it in its usual corner. He opened the kitchen door.

'Hello darling,' said his mum, 'How was school today?'

George stumbled backwards, placing the palms of his hands on the closing door behind him. 'What? What are *you* doing here?'

'What are you talking about?' she asked. 'Darling, is everything alright?' She walked over to him and placed the palm of her hand on his forehead. He shivered. 'You look a little peaky.'

'Oh er – yes. I'm fine, I'm well, I'm – just fine. I – I just don't understand?'

'Understand what?' asked his dad scratching his balding head, but not lifting it up out of the newspaper.

'This...'

'This what?' asked his mum. 'What is it darling?'

'Oh – er – it's nothing – ignore me.' George thought about this bizarre situation for a moment. He stared at his mum wide-eyed, trying to take it all in. Her shoulder-length brown hair was exactly as he remembered it, but a little greyer; the lines on her face were deeper, and there were more of them. But this was still his mum.

Then he realised. *This,* this must be what he wanted most in the world, for his mum to be at home, like she'd never left. This was just how his life would have been if she'd never disappeared.

George raised his eyes upwards. 'Thank you,' he whispered. To have the chance to spend 15 minutes more with his mum was something he had dreamt of a million times – because deep down he had truly believed that he would never see her again.

'What's that you're saying?' asked his dad.

'Oh nothing Dad – nothing at all. Mum – Mum are you OK?'

'Why yes George, I'm just fine. Why wouldn't I be?' she replied, serving up some home cooked jerk vegetables. 'I'm with my two favourite people in the world.'

'Oh I don't know,' said George, thinking back to that awful day – the day she'd disappeared. 'Maybe you'd rather be somewhere else.'

'George!' exclaimed his mum and dad together.

Dad frowned. 'What's got into you today? You're acting really weird.'

George cringed while his mum and dad stared at him. He didn't quite know what to say – I mean they thought all of this was normal – they didn't know that they were in his dreality.

'Nothing. Sorry.' George sat down at the table.

'I should think so too,' said his dad, folding his paper and putting it down to eat his dinner.

George stared at his mum. She was placing a napkin on her knee, she was smiling. He wanted to stare at her forever. But *no* – he couldn't – he remembered that this was only going to last for 15 minutes – and the time was passing by. There were things that he needed to find out. But he couldn't ask those questions – could he? Yes he could, yes he should.

'Tell me about the lift?' he asked quickly before he had a chance to change his mind.

He watched as his dad gagged on a piece of artichoke. His mum dropped her cutlery with a crash onto her plate.

So they did know. Why hadn't they told him? Stuart had been right.

'What?' gasped his mum.

'Tell me about the lift.'

Dad peered over the rim of his black glasses. 'What lift?'

'You know, the one at the station.'

'How do you know about the lift?' asked his mum slowly; her face had gone from pink to white.

'I found it.'

'Found it?' exclaimed his dad. 'How the hell did you find it?'

'I just did.'

Dad shook his head vigorously, his purple face turning violet. 'Look George, you're too young to know about any of this. It's much too dangerous. We'll tell you when you're older. Let's just forget you ever said anything and just enjoy our dinner.'

'I'm old enough to know now,' said George. 'Please – you've got to tell me.'

'No darling,' said his mum. 'Your father's right. We'll tell you when you're 16.'

'Well then I'll just have to get in it and see what happens.'

Mum and Dad gasped. 'George!'

'Well if that's the only way I'm going to find out...'

'You're stepping way out of line young man,' said Dad in a slow, deep voice.

'OK! OK!' said his mum, raising her hands. 'I'll tell you, but only because you're making it impossible for me not to.'

George could feel his hands getting clammy. He was about to be told the truth – about everything.

His dad got up from his chair and headed towards the door. He was shaking his head. 'I'm not sure about this Louisa. I'm really not.'

'Mum, please.'

George's mum looked at his dad. Dad shrugged his shoulders. His parting words were, 'If you must.' The door shut with a bit of a slam.

His mum adjusted herself in her chair and took a long, deep breath.

'Now darling, some of this may come as a bit of a shock, you see, that lift is very special.' She sat thoughtfully for a minute as if deciding where to start. 'Well, it was your Great, Great, Great Grandfather that first found the lift and realised its capabilities. You see, that lift is a form of transport, for our family, to other worlds – other worlds in other dimensions.'

'What do you mean other dimensions?'

'Other universes.'

'Wow, other universes, how mad is that. And is that the only way there?'

'Yes. Global Travellers are rare, most people don't have any way of getting to the other worlds, or maybe they just haven't been lucky enough to find their transportation vessel yet. But George, listen to me, you must promise that you'll wait until you're much older before you get into that lift. Like your father said, it can be dangerous.'

'Tell me about Leesome Shrouds.'

'George, how on earth do you know about that?'

'I must have read about it somewhere.'

'You can't have, I've been very careful not to write about any of this, and as far as I know no other Interglobal Traveller has either.'

'And Leesome Shrouds?' prompted George.

'Well – er, well, Leesome Shrouds,' she said, raising her eyes and smiling, 'is a wonderful place.'

'A place where you can wish for what you want,' said George.

'Why, yes George. But having material possessions isn't the most important thing in life – although you would think so looking at some of the wretchedly ill people there are there. I believe it's the people that you share your life with that are important. Making yourself ill over possessions only shortens the time you have with those people you love.'

'I don't believe you,' said George.

'What? Darling what are you talking about?'

'Why did you leave *me* then – all those years ago – and never come back.'

'Darling, what do you mean? I'm here with you now.'

'That's only because I'm in the Tunnel of Trances.'

His mum let out a bit of a shriek. 'What? I don't understand? The Tunnel of Trances, but – but George that's in Leesome Shrouds.'

'Yeah!'

'You mean you're in Leesome Shrouds right now?' said his mum, a look of white horror on her face. 'And you're in the Tunnel of Trances?'

'Yeah! This must be what I want most in the world – for my life to be back to normal – with you back at home.'

'OH NO! George! What did you mean when you said I left you?'

'You did leave. When I was seven.'

'Darling, I would never leave you. I love you,' she said, as she jumped up from her chair causing it to scrape along the floor.

Suddenly everything around George began to break up.

She cried out. 'We're running out of time.'

He watched as thin, red lines cracked across her face, breaking it apart. Like a china plate being smashed. She was shattering away and he could do nothing to stop it. Then all that remained was her voice, a distant whisper.

'George – something must have happened to me – I wouldn't leave you!'

George stretched out his arm. 'Mum! Please don't go. Not again!'

'Darling, I would never leave you. I promise you. *George – George I must be...*' But her voice dissolved into the vacant atmosphere, and she was gone.

'NO!' yelled George. 'Please – more time – please!'

Rippling images surrounded him.

What could she have meant – I must be – I must be what? Oh no. NO... I must be DEAD!

He knocked his shoulder on the wall as his quivering legs collapsed him to the ground. A chilling, ghostly shudder coursed under George's skin. His darting eyes smudged his vision – he rubbed them with the back of his hands. Unsteadily he raised himself up off the ground. He looked around. He was back in the corridor of the Tunnel of Trances. The front door to his home had vanished. He kicked the wall where it had been. The flames on the cavernous walls flickered aggressively. He needed to get out. His desperate legs dragged his feet along the floor as he made his way towards the exit. The hostile walls were choking him – he couldn't breathe.

He could see the ladder, in the distance. He staggered to it, his damp, trembling hands grasped onto it. He took in a deep breath and dropped his head. He stood still for a moment.

DEAD, she was *dead!*

But hadn't he always thought it possible that she could be dead, and that maybe she hadn't just run off? Yes, of course he had. But the police had never found a body, so he'd never quite wanted to believe it. So why was it such a shock to him now? Because now it was real – now he knew for sure.

-Chapter Seven-

THE DEMISE OF EDWIN BROWN

Daylight scorched George's eyes as he looked up. Molly and Peter were peering down at him.

'How was it George?' asked Peter, pulling him out of the hole. 'What did I tell you, isn't it great?'

'George, is everything alright?' said Molly. 'You look like you've seen a ghost!'

'I think I just have!'

'What? What are you talking about?'

'I need to sit down,' said George, stumbling over to a nearby wall.

Peter steadied him with his arm. 'George, what's happened?'

'My mum. My mum was in there.'

Molly looked at him kindly. 'What's so bad about that? That's good isn't it?'

'I asked her why she left?'

'And?'

'She told me that she would never leave me. That she loved me.'

'Well that's good isn't it?' asked Peter.

'Then she told me that she must be *Dead*.'

Peter and Molly looked at each other; he felt the atmosphere strain.

After a while Molly spoke up, 'I don't understand? She said that? That's a really weird thing to say, those were her exact words?'

'Yeah – well – no – not exactly, but she said "*I must be*" and then her voice just faded away.'

'Oh George,' said Molly, 'maybe she was going to say something else.'

'Like what?'

Molly paused for a moment. 'Like – oh er, I don't know. Like, I must be, er...'

'See! It couldn't be anything else. What am I going to do?'

'Come on George,' said Peter, 'I know what we'll do. We'll go and see Mum. She'll know what's happened here. Bet this sort of thing happens all the time, there'll be an explanation, I'm sure there will.'

'How can she help?' asked George.

Peter looked at his watch. 'She just knows loads of stuff – about loads of stuff. Come on, if we hurry we might catch her on her lunch break.'

They made their way to the offices where Mrs Hubbins worked as a counsellor for people with severe greening. George was praying that she would be able to help.

As they walked into Mrs Hubbins' office George felt something hard underfoot, at the same time he heard the sound of crunching ceramic.

'What's going on? That's the mug I bought Mum for her birthday!' shouted Peter.

George stared down at the shattered mug that lay on the floor, then ahead into the office. Shelves had been cleared of all books and paperwork, and the desk had been emptied of its contents, which lay on the floor. Even the drawers had been removed from their sockets.

'Aaaaaargh!' screamed Molly, covering her face with her hands. She stamped several times on the floor.

George looked around the room. There was something in the far corner. He squinted – he took in a sharp, jagged breath. 'What – what is it?'.

'It's a man,' said Molly, screwing her face up into a wrinkly ball. 'Aw what, I think he's been twisted! *Ugh!* Twisted to death.'

'*Pain!*' said George, his mouth dropping open and staying that way for quite some time. 'Ugh! Even his face has been twisted. Look, his chin's right round the other side of his face.'

The man stood tightly in the corner of the room, as if he had been trying to escape into the walls – his gaunt face pleading, bulging eyes full of old blood, discoloured, rusty. George could see where the bones had ripped through his clothes as they broke apart.

George's gaze made its way down to the man's patent leather shoes; there was a reflection of his twisted body in them.

'Who is it?' asked Peter.

'You know – it – sorry, I mean *he,* looks a bit like Edwin Brown,' said Molly.

'You know, I think you're right,' said Peter walking right up to him. 'I think it is Edwin.'

Molly shook her head. 'Oh not Edwin Brown. Poor Edwin. Oh no, his poor family.'

Peter turned round, blood draining from his face. 'If he has been twisted to death, then where's the other body?'

George jumped. '*Other body?*' He looked behind him. 'What do you mean – other body?'

Molly said. 'Well someone's obviously *wished* this on him, because you couldn't do this by hand, could you? So to do a wish this big would mean that you'd die from greening straight away. So there should be a body, somewhere close by.'

'What if it's your mum's body?' said George, not thinking.

'George!' shouted Peter. 'As if things aren't bad enough without you making it worse.'

'Sorry,' said George, realising what he'd just said. 'I'm not thinking straight, what with everything that's happened, what with *my* mum and all.'

'Look,' said Molly. 'Let's get out of here, something's not right. No body? Someone must have moved it, they could still be around. They might be dangerous.'

'But what if George is right and it is my mum's body. What if Mum's dead?'

'Don't say things like that!' said Molly. 'She'll be fine. Look she's probably just gone to get help.'

George didn't think that was going to be the case.

'Look for Mum's work diary, it'll say who her last appointment was with, then we'll know who was the last person to see her.'

Then George realised that right now he and Peter had something terrible in common – neither of them knew whether their mum was alive or *dead.*

George felt his legs shake, he picked up a chair that had been knocked over and sat in it. He sighed. This was all such a mess. He gazed at the empty locations of the missing drawers – there was a compartment at the back of the desk with a small handle. Bending over he plunged his arm into the space. He pulled out an official looking black book. Firmly printed in gold letters was the word DIARY.

'Hey, look at this,' he shouted. 'The diary.' George opened it at the first page. There was nothing written on it, he thumbed through all the pages. He could feel Molly peering over his shoulder.

She sighed. 'It's blank, it's all blank.' She did an enormous sniff right down George's ear.

George shook his head. 'But why would she hide a blank book? It doesn't make sense.'

Peter said. 'None of this does, come on let's get out of here, and bring *that* diary, and some of those files. We should leave right now, we might not be safe.'

They hurriedly gathered all the files they could manage to carry, and left the wreck of an office behind. They were half way home when Molly let out a small shriek. She stopped dead. 'I've only gone and left my bag in the office. I'll have to go back for it.'

Peter shook his head. 'No Molly. You're not going back, it's too dangerous. You'll just have to do without it for a bit.'

'I can't,' she snapped, 'it's got all my make-up in it. I need it.'

'It's just a bit of make-up,' said Peter. 'You can do without it for a bit can't you? Anyway you wear way too much.'

'No I don't!' she snapped. 'You know nothing, I need it.' And she turned around and stormed off.

George looked at Peter to see what they should do. 'Oh just let her go, there's no stopping her when she's like that.'

They walked quickly back to the house where George busied himself with the blank diary. He felt something from it, that it was hiding something, something important.

Ten minutes had passed when eventually he cracked it. *'Take a look at this!'* And then he slid the spine upwards and away from the book.

'What is it?' said Peter walking over.

'I bet this fits in these ridges here!' said George, pointing to the part of the book that had previously opened. He carefully placed the spine between the ridges and pushed it down – he heard a click. He opened the book where the spine used to be. There was writing inside.

'George you're a genius. Go to her last appointment.'

2011 DIARY
09.00	Mrs Louisa Price
10.00	Sir Augustine
11.30	Lunch
14.00	Mr and Mrs Adams

'What? Oh my God,' yelled George. 'It can't be!'

'I know,' said Peter shaking his head. 'Sir Augustine! What's going on?'

George pointed to the first entry, 'No, not that, *this*!'

'What about it?'

'That! That's my mum's name,' said George, feeling an ice-cold shudder crawl right through him.

'What?'

George flicked viciously through the pages. 'No, it can't be my mum – can it? What would she be doing here, and what would she be doing meeting your mum?'

'Look George, it's probably just a coincidence. There's probably hundreds of people with that name.'

George sighed. 'Yeah I suppose.'

'Nothing to get worked up about then.'

'But hang on, it's not dead common is it?' said George. 'I mean how many Louisa Price's do you know?'

Peter looked thoughtful for a moment. 'Well none, but...'

'See,' said George. 'Maybe the Tunnel of Trances was wrong. What if she's alive and she's here?'

'George calm down! You're jumping to conclusions.'

But George couldn't calm down. This *had* to be his mum – he felt it. It was too much of a coincidence – wasn't it? He carried on desperately searching through the diary for something else – a clue – an address – just something. Finally he tossed the notebook aside. 'Nothing. Not a single thing. Look I need to find out whether this is my mum, so we need to find *your* mum, then I can ask her.'

'Yes George,' said Peter sarcastically. 'We *do* need to find my mum, you're right.'

'Oh yeah, sorry. So what do we do now?'

There was a moment's silence, then, 'We should go to the library, yes that's it, then we can find out where this Louisa

Price lives and Sir Augustine too, and then we can pay them both a visit.'

'OK,' said George.

'After all they're our two main suspects so we might as well concentrate on them.'

For the first time George realised that what Peter was saying was true. If this Louisa Price was his mum, then she was a suspect. She could be the one responsible for Mrs Hubbins' disappearance, even Edwin Brown's death; after all he didn't know who his mum was any more. He knew that he had adored her, looked up to her, loved her when he was young, but if this woman *was* her, who was she now and why had she never come home? It was all so confusing – was his mum dead – alive – guilty – innocent – here? One thing for sure, he was going to find out.

Peter interrupted his thoughts. 'We'll go as soon as Molz gets back.'

It wasn't long until Molly came bursting through the door. 'Guess who I've just seen? Only Sir Augustine, that's who, he was in your mum's office.'

Peter frowned. 'But his appointment with her was hours ago, I don't understand. Did you ask him what he was doing there?'

'You're joking aren't you?' said Molly. 'Sir Augustine, speak to the likes of me? Anyway listen, he was on the phone, so I accidently listened in.'

'Go on.'

'Wait till you hear this.' Molly looked kind of pleased with herself. 'I heard him telling someone that the Blood Ghost has been destroyed – "*splattered*" – he said.'

George flinched at the disturbing image that flashed through his mind. 'The Blood Ghost! What's that?'

'It guards the Crux,' said Peter, frowning even harder now. George noticed that he'd gone a grey shade of pale. 'But I don't understand. You can't destroy The Blood Ghost, not unless you want to die a disgusting, horrible death yourself; you'd have to be mad!'

'I know,' said Molly. 'It's crazy isn't it? And Sir Augustine said that the Crux has been taken!'

'*Oh no, Molz!*'

'I know!'

'What's The Crux?' asked George.

'Unimaginable power is what it is – wishes without consequence – that sort of thing,' said Molly.

George had a thought. 'Hey, maybe it was that man in your mum's office that destroyed the Blood Ghost, his death looked pretty disgusting to me.'

Peter was shaking his head. 'What Edwin? No way, he wouldn't even say *boo* to a ghost, let alone kill one.'

'It doesn't change anything for us though does it?' asked George. 'I mean the Crux going missing.'

'No,' said Peter. 'We'll just stick to the plan and go to the library. But this is bad, bad news. Leesome Shrouds is in big trouble.'

-Chapter Eight-

THE LIBRARIA

The library was an immense skyscraper, with thousands of intricate mouldings of every colour imaginable on the outside. There were dragons, goblins, monsters, vampires, werewolves and zombies stretching way up into the sky.

'Now that's amazing,' said George.

'Isn't it?' said Molly. 'They're all characters from books, every book ever written. Look, there's Snow White and the eight dwarves.'

'Seven,' said George.

'No – eight.'

'Come on you two,' said Peter. 'Never mind that.'

They walked in through the huge wooden doors.

'I can't see the ceiling, it's miles away,' said George. 'And books, it's just books all the way to the top. How do you get them down from all the way up there?'

'You have to get one of the Librarias to help you,' replied Molly. 'There's one, over there.'

George looked over and saw the strangest, tallest human being he had ever seen. Humungous pointy ears, a tiny hole for a mouth and huge protruding eyes. Then another similar one walked passed him, carrying about 50books in her arms. Each Libraria wore a long black gown and a small black cap.

'They're from the City of Libraria, that's why they all look similar,' explained Molly. 'They make ideal book workers because of their strength, and the fact that they can hear someone whispering from 20 metres away.'

'SSSSSHHHHHHHHH!' came a harsh and surprisingly loud voice from behind. George turned to find a stern looking Libraria glaring at them.

Molly mouthed the word sorry, and the Libraria continued on her intellectual way. They picked their way through the tables and chairs and sat down at an available desk. Peter got two order forms and handed one to George. 'Just write your name at the top, and your mum's in the enquiry section.'

George did as he said. Peter filled out his enquiry, requesting the whereabouts of Sir Augustine's house. They signalled over to a Libraria and handed the pieces of paper to her. The Libraria took the paper to a central station and handed it to another Libraria with even more googly eyes.

Peter's reply was first back. 'Got it. He lives at number one, Avaricious Avenue, Leesome Falls. Should be easy enough to find.'

George looked over towards the Libraria. The request that he had handed in seemed to be causing a bit of a commotion. Within minutes the three of them were surrounded.

'Come with us,' said one of the Libraria without moving her mouth.

Slowly George and the others got to their feet. What had they – *he* – done wrong? The Librarias glided along the floor as they clumsily followed. They were taken into a room where three super efficient looking Librarias sat behind a desk.

'Come this way,' beckoned the middle one with a long, crinkly forefinger.

'Look, what's this about?' asked Molly impressively. 'We haven't done anything wrong. I've a good mind to walk out of here right now.'

'STAY WHERE YOU ARE!' screeched a commanding voice from one of the Libraria. Just which one it was George couldn't tell. 'You have been brought before us because Edwin Brown has been found murdered. He has been wished to death.'

'We know,' said Molly. 'We found him earlier today.'

'And you didn't think to alert the authorities?'

They all remained quiet.

'Are we correct in saying that you knew this Edwin Brown?'

'Yes,' said Molly.

'Except George, he didn't know him,' said Peter.

'Which one of you killed him?'

Molly gasped in horror. 'None of us.'

'We *couldn't* have wished him dead like that,' said Peter. 'And you know that, because one of us would be dead too – from greening.'

'This is true, but you have someone with you that may not be affected by greening. *He* may have killed him!'

It took a few seconds for it to dawn on George that they were referring to him. 'What? Me? I wouldn't kill anyone!'

'But George *is* affected by greening,' insisted Molly. 'He was as sick as a Beazlefriar the other day when he'd overwished at the E. House.'

'Nonetheless we cannot take your word for it,' said one. 'We will have to run some tests on this *Being* to see if he differs from us. Ten Foot Two and Ten Foot One, take this Being to the experimental chamber. Get Twelve Foot Three to run the tests. Oh and let the Wish Doctor know, I'm sure he'll be very interested in this procedure.'

George felt his arms being pulled behind his back. He tried to wriggle free but couldn't. He could feel his legs being lifted off the ground.

'NO!' he yelled, and tried to break free. But it was no use. They strapped his arms down onto a trolley and pushed him down a long corridor, his mind a-boggle with images of what was going to happen to him. He was taken to a very white room and left alone, still strapped to the trolley. He had heard one of the Librarias say something about sterilising the equipment. He really needed to get out of here, and quick, before they did find out that he wasn't affected by wishing. And what would happen then? He would probably be charged with Edwin Brown's murder. He would probably go to prison, or even worse get shot or hung. He had to escape, and quick. Maybe he should just wish himself out. No, transportation wishes – they didn't work. But what would help him get out? There had to be something.

That was it, he would wish for pointy ears and huge eyes, a tall slim body and an unflattering outer garment. Then he could walk around undetected and rescue his friends. After untying himself from the trolley he set about transforming himself into a Libraria. When George wished to be taller he could feel his bones stretching inside him. He wanted to cry out with the pain, especially when he felt his eyeballs being sucked out of their sockets. But to shout out would be the end for him, so he bore the pain.

Eventually he was standing in front of a mirror he had wished for, looking just like a Libraria, although he had made himself a little better looking than most of the ones he had seen.

Just then he heard voices approaching. He quickly rushed over to stand behind the door. He could hear a key turning. The door swung open and in walked two Libraria. One was carrying what George could only assume was a torture device. They rushed over to the trolley and examined the broken straps.

'Where is he?' shouted one of them.

'Oh no, he has escaped!'

'STOP right there, Eight Foot Nothing?'

George froze.

'What's happened to the boy?'

George realised they were talking to him. He turned around and said in the shrillest voice he could manage 'I don't know, I just came in and he was gone. We need to get help!' George hoped that his voice would fool them.

'Quite right. Send out a red alert. We shouldn't have too much trouble locating him, hideous looking thing like that.'

George felt himself go red. 'Are the others safely locked away?'

'Yes they're on the twenty-first floor in the Chief Libraria's office. They won't escape from there.'

'Come on let's go and look for him,' said the other Libraria.

Now all George needed to do was to get to the others. He found a lift. There were four Libraria in it. He reached over and pushed button 21. They each raised their eyebrows. He pretended he hadn't noticed anything, dipped his head and continued to stare uncomfortably at the lift floor. By the time he had got to the eighth floor George was all alone. Up and up it went, until finally it pinged on floor 21.

There was a door at either end of the corridor; he took a right turn. There was a plaque on the door: DISCIPLINARY ROOM. No wonder the people in the lift were giving him funny looks. He opened the door. It was dark inside. He flicked on the light switch. The room smelt like rotten meat. On the walls were lots of posters showing various medical procedures. He walked hesitantly into the room to inspect the pictures more closely. If he wasn't mistaken it looked like these Libraria people were taking inches from their height as a means of disciplining. The smaller they were the lower ranking in the library they were. George walked over to a huge plastic container; he opened it up, his head wrenched backwards.

He had been right about the smell. The bin was full of rotting skin and bone shavings. He felt dizzy – he had to get out – get out now. He made his way out of the door and along the corridor, his stomach lurching. He staggered to the door at the far end. CHIEF LIBRARIA'S OFFICE. He tried the door. It was locked.

'Molly, Peter, are you in there?' he shouted.

Molly's voice. 'George is that you?'

'Yeah, I've manage to escape. Open the door.'

After much fiddling about with the lock on the other side, the door was opened. Molly took one look at George and took a step back. 'We weren't trying to escape or anything. Why would we? I mean you'd find us in a second. We were, er, just going to stretch our legs.'

Peter stepped forward. 'What've you done with George?'

'It's me stupid,' said George.

'No way! Is it really?' asked Peter prodding him/her in the side. 'That's mad!'

'Oh no!' said Molly, a look of concern spread across her face. 'George, that's a huge wish, to change yourself like that. You're going to be so sick tomorrow and it'll probably knock about five years off your life – long term I mean.'

'I'll be OK,' said George quite touched that she cared. 'Now come on let's get out of here.'

Molly looked at him admiringly. 'What's the plan?'

'How about if anyone asks, I'm having to move you because I – and by that I mean me – I mean *George,* has escaped.'

'That'll do it,' said Peter.

Soon they were in an empty lift. It didn't stop until the eleventh floor. Two Librarias got in.

'What's this, what's going on?' one demanded.

'I am taking them to a secret location,' replied George in a screechy voice. 'Under strict orders from the Chief. That revolting little thing called George has not been found yet so the Chief thinks that this is the wisest thing to do.'

'Yes, it seems like he has just vanished,' said one of them. 'But we will find him. He's probably cowering in some corner or other, that's why we can't hear him. He'll come out soon enough.'

Several explanations later they were on the ground floor and heading towards the door. They could just about smell the fresh air when they heard a scream. 'STOP!'

They turned around to see the tallest Libraria they had ever seen. George estimated that she must be at least 15 foot high.

'GET THEM!'

'RUN!' screamed Molly.

They ran through the doors before anyone could stop them, and they ran, and ran a bit further. People in the streets gasped in surprise when they saw George.

'They think you're a Libraria. You never see them outside of the library,' said Molly panting. 'They're only ever really seen in the town of Libraria itself, hardly ever in Leesome Shrouds.'

They ran some more.

'Stop,' gasped George eventually. He could feel his overstretched bones rubbing on his skin as he ran, and it was beginning to cause him severe pain. 'Stop. I can't go any further, my bones and these shoes, these shoes are killing me.'

He slumped onto a nearby front doorstep, and took off his high-heeled shoes. He rubbed his aching feet.

'Don't take them off George,' said Peter laughing. 'They really suit you.'

George picked up one of the shoes, and laughing too, threw it at him.

'Stop it you two!' said Molly looking grim.

'What?'

'Think about it.'

What with everything that had happened in the library George had almost forgotten about the awful situation he was in. He looked over at Peter, who too had gone quiet. 'Molly's right, Peter. We're here laughing and joking when both our mums could be dead.'

Peter nodded shamefully. 'Well we need to find out one way or another don't we? I say we pay Sir Augustine a visit.'

'But how are we going to get Sir Augustine to see us,' said Molly. 'He's such a big star we'll never get close. I read all about him in *More Than OK* magazine last month, and it showed pictures of where he lives – it's like this huge castle by the sea, with guards and everything.'

'She's right you know,' said Peter. 'The guards will stop us getting to him.'

'Then we'll just have to find a way to get past them,' said George.

'But even if we do get past them, then there's the gates. They're about ten metres high,' said Molly.

'Can't we just wish them open?' said George.

'Won't work,' said Molly, shaking her head. 'Thing about keys is you need to know there exact shape for the wish to work.'

'Oh right,' said George.

'I've got a bit of an idea though,' said Molly thoughtfully. 'Might be a bit of a long shot, but it could be worth a go.'

'Go on, Molz.'

'My mum and dad might have a key. To the gates I mean.'

'You what?' said Peter with a bit of an edge to his voice.

Molly raised her eyes. 'I know, but hear me out. See they were given this key in a presentation case, it's the Master Key – to Leesome Shrouds.'

Peter shook his head. 'Still don't understand.'

'They were given it because of all the stuff they've donated to charity over the years.'

'Charity!' snarled Peter screwing his face up. '*Your* mum and dad – never.'

George was thinking that perhaps Peter was being a bit harsh.

'I know,' said Molly laughing, but in a nasty kind of way. 'Mad isn't it. What no one knew was that it was me and Mark who had done all the wishing. It was us who had been sick for charity, not Mum and Dad.'

'Who's Mark?'

'My little brother.'

'But why did you overwish for charity?' asked George.

'Because they made us.'

'What do you mean they made you?'

'Mum and Dad have got an obsession with collecting things, but they don't like to wish for them themselves, because it makes them sick. So they get me and Mark to do it for them. Sometimes we say no, because we know it'll make us dead ill, that's when they lock us up in the cellar. It's so cold down there they know that we'll agree to do it in the end.'

'No wonder you don't want to spend any time at home.'

'I suppose you kind of get used to it after a while, the sickness I mean,' said Molly, shrugging her shoulders. 'Your body sort of becomes a bit immune I suppose. So what do you think, about the key I mean, maybe it's just what we need? And it'll give me a chance to check on Mark.'

Peter was nodding his head. 'I think it's definitely worth a go.'

'There's just one problem I can see,' said Molly. 'There's no way they'll let us have it so we'll have to sort of *borrow* it for a while, if you know what I mean.'

'Come on then,' said George. 'Let's get going.'

'It's way too late now,' said Peter looking at his watch. 'We'll have to go and borrow it first thing in the morning.'

-Chapter Nine-

MARK

George woke up the following morning with a stiff neck. He pulled a box out from under his head. He pushed it back onto the pile, and stared at all the boxes. There must have been 200 of them. What had he been thinking – he hadn't been thinking, he just hadn't been able to stop. He wouldn't even be able to bring most of them home with him. He supposed he could give them to his new friends, but then that would mean he'd have to tell them about everything – and he didn't know whether he could quite trust them enough yet.

But for now, he knew one thing, and that was that he needed to look sick again after the Libraria wish. He reached into his pocket, took out the packet and looked thoughtfully at the pills. He couldn't face taking three again – he would take two, and make up some excuse.

He went downstairs where the others were having breakfast.

'Feeling rough?' asked Peter frowning.

'You could say that.'

'You're going to suffer today,' said Peter, clenching his teeth. 'Transformation – that's a massive wish. Mind you, you don't look half as bad as I thought you would.'

'No you don't,' said Molly eyeing him suspiciously.

'Dad's gone out with a search party,' said Peter, 'but I think they're wasting their time. I think our investigation is much better. We're setting off to Molly's in a minute, don't suppose you're up to it though are you George?'

'Yeah, I'm definitely coming with you,' said George, feeling a rumble in his stomach, and immediately regretting taking any pills at all. 'I'll be OK, I think.'

'You sure George?' said Molly. 'I mean you probably shouldn't even be out of bed.'

'Yeah, I'm sure.'

'Come on then,' said Molly. 'But I honestly don't know how you're doing it.'

The streets were strangely quiet, and George felt a weird tension in the air.

'Is it just me or does something not feel right?' said Molly five minutes into their journey.

'Yeah,' said Peter. 'And what's that humming noise? And where is everyone?'

The humming turned into voices, voices that grew louder.

'What was that?' asked George. 'Listen.'

'Someone's screaming,' said Molly.

'It's coming from Green Park,' said Peter quickening his step.

'What's Green Park?' asked George.

'The place where most of the green people live,' said Peter. 'I'm going to live there when I'm older. The houses are amazing, honestly George you should see...'

A terrific explosion came from round the corner jolting them to a halt. They stood still for a moment listening to the crashes and the yelling that came from around the corner.

'I think we should turn back,' said Molly.

'No,' said Peter. 'We need to get the key, and if we have to go all the way round it'll take us ages.'

George could feel his heart pounding, and his legs began to shake. He thought it best if they went the longer way round, but chose not to say anything just yet. He didn't want to look soft.

Down the street and turning the corner George saw a sight he knew he would never forget.

A leafy green park.

Dozens of boys – men. Blood, kicking, fists. Smacking, crunching, smashing – screams oozing down the streets – gore!

Women – girls cowering down alleyways, screaming at them to stop.

Noise – conflict – hurt.

A glass bottle smashed at the side of George.

'What's happening?' demanded Peter, grabbing the arm of a man walking past.

'Wot shud av appened years ago,' shouted the man punching his fist into the air. 'Us pure uns are sortin out those green uns.'

The man's face was snarling, showing his yellow teeth.

George felt his hands clench at his side. He took a step backwards.

'What do you mean,' asked Molly, 'sorting um out?'

'It's them green uns that's taken the Crux and splattered the Blood Ghost *and* probably killed that Edwin Brown,' said the man. 'We should've never given um rights, should've sorted um out years ago, then this wud never av appened.'

Peter gasped. 'You can't do this, no one deserves this.'

'Greed is all they care about, every single one of um.'

Molly yelled out. 'That's not true!' Her voice was trembling, she began to shake.

'Some of our friends live here,' shouted Peter.

The man leaned over, squaring his face up to Peter's 'Well go over to their side then if you feel like that, you green loving son of a...'

'*Come on Peter*,' shouted Molly grabbing the sleeve of his coat. 'Let's go, we need to go, *come on*.' She pulled again at his coat, this time a lot harder.

'But some of our friends might be getting hurt, they might need our help.'

'Peter there's nothing we can do. *We* could all get hurt, and that's not going to help us find your mum is it? Come on, now, we need to get away from here.'

George agreed. 'Molly's right, we need to concentrate on finding our mums.'

'OK, OK!' said Peter. 'But this is all wrong.'

The three of them turned and walked away.

The journey to Molly's was a long tense one, and when they arrived they found that her mum and dad were in for the day and that was that.

'What are we going to do?' asked George.

Peter shrugged his shoulders, 'I suppose one of us needs to distract them.' He turned to face Molly.

'Oh no! There's no way I'm going in there on my own. No way.'

Peter nodded, 'Well what if I go in with you, and George sneaks into the cellar. That might work.'

George wasn't sure.

'OK,' said Molly.

George sighed, 'What do you want me to do?'

'Right,' said Molly. She began to explain to George the layout of the living room and the location of the cellar door. 'And the key's in a glass box down there somewhere. OK?'

'Have you got all that George?'

He nodded reluctantly. 'Think so.'

'Here,' said Peter holding out his hand palm upright. He closed his eyes for a second. A yellow plastic torch appeared. He gave it to George. 'It's dark down there.'

'Great!'

Molly pulled a key out of her pocket, 'Come on then, let's get this over with. I'll just pretend to fall over or something, then you get past, but be as quick as you can, I'm not spending any more time in there than I have to. So if you don't get that key in less than half an hour we're leaving without you.'

Charming thought George, and what kind of people was she threatening to leave him with exactly?

Molly turned the key and walked into the house with Peter, leaving the door slightly ajar. George peered through the gap and waited for the signal.

'Hello Aunty Jean, Uncle Ralph,' said Peter, as he carefully picked his way through all the tat that lay around the room.

'What you doing here?' demanded Mr Coddle, who was sitting in a flowery armchair, suspiciously leering over some tinted spectacles. 'What do you want?' He was a tall, skinny man with a large head that was bald in parts. He was wearing a cheap T-shirt and grey jogging bottoms.

'Oh – er, well we just called around to...' began Peter.

Just then, there came a theatrical *bang*. Molly had hurled herself onto the floor and lay in a heap at the side of her mum. Mr and Mrs Coddle jumped up in shock and stared unsympathetically at their daughter.

'Molly Coddle!' screamed Mrs Coddle. 'Get up of that floor – now! You almost frightened me to death.'

George was sure he heard Molly say, 'if only,' under her breath.

Mrs Coddle was a stoutly built lady with a small head. She had on the same jogging bottoms as her husband, though in a much larger size.

Molly managed to make enough of a commotion getting up from the floor to allow George to walk right behind her parents. He looked for the trap door Molly had described. There it was, just as she'd said. He tiptoed over, listening to them all arguing. He grabbed hold of the large iron loop and lifted up the door slowly. There were some steps going down into the dankness.

George lifted up the hatch. The last thing he heard was Molly asking where Mark was.

'Outside playing. Not that it's any of your...'

George silently pulled the hatch down behind him, turned on the torch and descended into a sinister silence. George cringed as a spider's web brushed across his face. He followed the circle of dusty grey from the torch down to the bottom, and pulled his jacket around him tightly. He trembled, he had always imagined this was the kind of place his mum's body would be found. He pushed himself over to a pile of objects and began to rummage through them. He could hear footsteps up above, and muffled shouting.

Then a noise, from the furthest part of the cellar. The first thought to enter George's head was RATS. He would freak if there were rats down here. Quickly he shone his torch over – he jumped as a huge pair of luminescent eyes glared at him. He let out a yell.

A commotion from up above. George turned off his torch and held his breath. The hatch lifted up and a beam of light came down from above. It reached to the tip of George's trainer. Molly's face appeared at the hatch. 'Is Mark down there?'

What was she doing, she was going to ruin everything.

Mrs Coddle's voice, 'No he's not, and it's none of your damn business anyway, you don't even live here most of the time, so what's it got to do with you?'

A hand grabbed hold of Molly's shoulder and dragged her back.

'Let me see,' she shouted.

George could hear a bit of a struggle, then the hatch went down. He turned his torch back on, and slowly moved it back towards the glaring eyes. They were still there, just staring at him. 'Are you Mark?'

A sad, weak voice came out of the darkness. 'Yeah.'

George made his way over to him. He could see a boy of about seven leaning over an old, yellow bucket. He couldn't help thinking about everything Molly had told him about her parents making them overwish.

A diluted whisper. 'Who are you?'

'I'm George, a friend of your sister's.' He pulled over a crate and quietly sat down.

'Why are you down here?'

'Mum and Dad wanted me to wish for a gold statue of Sir Augustine for them.' Mark took in a gasp. 'They'd seen it in *Wish* magazine, but it was 33 wishes so I knew I'd be dead ill and I just couldn't face any more chucking up. So I said no – and here I am – again.'

'OK.'

'Why are you here?'

'Molly said your mum and dad have the Master Key down here,' said George. 'But that doesn't matter now. What matters is that we get you out of here.'

Mark raised his arm slowly and pointed towards a broken wooden chest in the far corner of the cellar. George tiptoed over, lifted up the lid and rummaged around. Eventually he held up a large golden key. It was in a glass frame on a backing of red velvet. 'This it?'

Mark nodded.

'Great,' said George. 'Now come on, let's get out of here.' George put his arm around Mark and carefully got him to stand up. A cold looking grey blanket fell from his legs. They made their way to the trap door. George lifted it up far enough to see what was going on in the living room.

Molly was still trying to get past her mum to get to the trap door. 'You said he was out playing, but he's in there isn't he? Just let him out of there please. Look, whatever it is you want, I'll do it, I'll wish for it.'

'No!' said Mrs Coddle in a voice that could curdle water. 'He needs to be taught a lesson. Can't have his own way all the time.'

'Own way?' shouted Molly. 'You've got to be joking.'

'Enough of your lip,' shouted her dad bashing her about her head.

'Yeah,' agreed her mum. 'Now get out! Throw them out Ralph. Coming round here snooping.'

Mr Coddle grabbed Molly forcibly by her arm and dragged her across the living room pushing her out into the street. Peter held up his hands and followed her out.

'Now get lost the pair of you, and don't come back!' he shouted slamming the door.

George let the hatch drop. He looked at Mark who was propping himself up against the wall. 'Oh no, they've just thrown Molly and Peter out, how are we going to get out now?'

Mark shrugged, wearily.

'Well we'll have to think of something quickly because we need to get over to Sir Augustine's before it gets dark.'

'What for?'

'Your aunt's gone missing. Peter's mum I mean. We're trying to find her.'

Mark raised his head. 'Not Aunty Anne, she's my favourite.' He paused for a moment. 'I know a way out.'

'What?'

'I'll just tell them that I'll wish for them, then they'll take me into the kitchen, as they always do, then you can get out.'

'No way, I'm not letting you do that.'

'I want to do it for Aunty Anne.'

'Yeah, but...'

'It's alright,' said Mark shrugging. 'I'll have to do it in the end anyway, so I might as well do it now.' Mark raised his left hand, 'You might want to stand further back for a minute.' He pulled his hand back – hesitated – took a deep breath – bent his head – took another deep breath, then gave five loud knocks.

'What are you doing?' said George in a high-pitched whisper.

'Special knock, means I'm ready to wish.'

George stepped further back into the cellar. The trap door opened. George saw a couple of arms extend down towards Mark. They hauled him out. The hatch went down. George went over and lifted it up again.

'Just had a visit from your sister. Don't know who she thinks she is. Proper little madam – not like you – like our good little boy eh?' said Mr Coddle.

Mrs Coddle put her arm around him. 'Now *son*. Let's get you something to eat. You know it's not good to wish on an empty stomach.' And they guided him out of the room and towards the kitchen.

Now was George's chance to escape. But he couldn't leave Mark here like this. But then again there was nothing he could do on his own. Maybe the others would have a plan. But for now he had to get out. He went up the remaining steps, closed down the hatch and sneaked over to the front door. Glancing over to the kitchen, he shuddered as he watched them give Mark a slice of dry bread. George shook his head, then stepped out into the street.

Molly was pacing up and down, and looking ferocious. 'I know it was my idea but we should never have come here. Bad, bad idea.'

George saw her clenching her fists behind her back.

'I know,' said Peter kicking a nearby wall. 'It's just so annoying.'

'Come on,' said Molly. 'I need to get away from here. Well away.'

'But what about your brother?' said George. 'We have to help him.'

Molly shook her head and frowned. 'Don't you get it? There's nothing we can do.'

But George didn't get it, not really, 'They shouldn't be allowed to do this.'

'They're his mum and dad, they can do what they want!'

-Chapter Ten-

THE SECURITY

The underbus trip to Leesome Falls was a quiet one, and the incident at Molly's was never spoken about again. George could feel an emotion – a tension so grotesque it made him feel sicker than he was sure four sickness tablets would have made him feel. He could tell the others were feeling it too. The silence was only broken by Peter telling them that the next stop was theirs.

They trudged off the underbus, and up some dingy steps to the street above.

'This way,' said Peter, looking at the map he had wished for.

He stopped dead at the corner of an old, grey building. Held out his arm to stop them going any further. 'Just around this corner. I'll just check it out. He peered around the corner, then turned to face Molly. 'There's no way we'll get in, why didn't you say his house was guarded by Skullduffers?'

'Because I didn't know, it just said that his house was guarded.'

'Well this has been a complete waste of time,' said Peter. 'Might as well just go home.'

George wanted to see what a Skullduffer was, so he craned his neck around the corner. By some large black wrought iron gates stood a man, must have reached up eight foot, easy. He was wearing a really smart black suit, bow tie and had slicked back, black hair. Deadly eyes. But what was *that?* George strained his eyes. Yes, he could see it now. A flesh coloured horn-like thing, *big*, coming out of the man's forehead, curving upwards. 'What the Hell's that?'

Peter asked, 'What?'

'That thing on his head.'

Peter screwed his face up, '*Pain* is what that is.'

'What do you mean, pain?'

'Skullduffer horn, look at the end of it, cuts through skin and bone dead easy. Wouldn't fancy getting a stab from that would you?'

George imagined his flesh being gashed open, and his bones splintering apart. He was sure his heart began to shake. Maybe they were taking things too far. 'And what's that stick thing he keeps knocking against his leg? Looks like a baseball bat.'

'A golden cosh?' said Peter. 'To batter you with, not that he'd need it. I mean look at the size of him. But it's got special powers just in case, it makes him even more powerful.'

A rustling came from over to George's right. The Skullduffer looked over to his left. Another Skullduffer came into view, though this one was considerably shorter. George reckoned he was about five foot six at the most. He was wearing a shabby, faded suit and a cream coloured shirt that George could tell had once been white. About five of the buttons were open at the top. George could just about make out a faded tattoo of barbed wire around his neck, and a thick gold chain bounced off his podgy chest. His horn was jaggedly snapped off at the top, and his nose was spread right across his face, like a trodden-on plum. He'd obviously had it broken several times. He walked up to the other Skullduffer and looked up. 'Joey *The Rhino* Milano – respect my man.' He held up his hand for a high five, that didn't come. Silence for a moment, while Joey looked him up and down, way more down than up.

'Duffer Don isn't it? Not seen you for a while.'

'Been in the slammer for six months for assault on a minor. Only broke the little sod's kneecap, nothing else. Well a few bruises that's all, black eye that sort of thing, oh and a bit of a ripped...'

'Yeah yeah,' said Joey, raising one eyebrow. 'I get the picture. So you didn't think to pick on someone your own age then?'

'Well yeah but no one around, fancied a bit of a scrap, you know how it goes.'

'No not really.'

'They've only just let me out you know. The Dibble made me come straight here, got to do this for my community service every day for the next two years. Bit harsh don't you think? I mean I've already done my time.'

Joey just shrugged.

'Anyway what the Helcrix are you doing here Joey?'

Silence. A hard stare.

'Sorry – er I mean, Joey *The Rhino* Milano.'

'Got done for possession. Caught with five kilos of wishing liquor on me. Got a good brief though, she got me off on a technicality. I've only got to do 100 hours. One more shift should do it.'

'That's good. So what's been going on while I've been banged up?'

'The Great White Sapphire's been taken.'

Duffer Don inhaled sharply. 'What do you mean taken? How do you take something the size of a palace?'

'Don't know – it just disappeared,' said Joey, buttoning up a long navy coat right up to under his chin. 'Everyone showed up for work yesterday and it was gone. Completely disappeared. Must be the person with the Crux, no one else has that kind of power. Anyway I'm off now, see my kids.'

'How many you got?'

Joey almost smiled. 'Just two. Yeah, Little Duct Tape – she's nearly one, and Lenny *Little Rhino* Milano – well he's fighting like a bad man already and he's only two and a half.'

'Smart eh? Like his dad.'

'Yeah. I'm dead proud.'

Joey handed his cosh to Duffer Don.

George was sure he saw it change colour from golden to a muck-ish brown.

'Well, probably see you around,' said Duffer Don.

'Hope not,' said Joey, turning – walking away – not looking back.

Duffer Don lowered his head.

Peter punched the air. 'Yes! It's got to be easier to get past now, just look at him, he's a wreck. Maybe we should just jump him, I reckon between us we could overpower him.'

'Not while he's got that cosh,' said Molly.

George stared at the brown stick. 'Well what'll we do then?'

'We'll have to distract him,' said Peter.

George thought it was hopeless. 'So how are we going to do that?'

Peter shrugged, 'No idea. Anyone got any ideas?'

George shook his head. How would he know what to do, he hadn't even known what a Skullduffer was until five minutes ago. And that cosh might be real dangerous.

'Well there is one thing,' said Molly eventually.

'What?'

She shook her head hard. 'Oh it doesn't matter, I shouldn't have said anything.'

'Come on Molz, you can't do that. Tell us.'

'Well I've heard – oh it's probably nothing.'

'Come on Molz. We need all the help we can get, so if you know something you'd better tell us now.'

'Well it's – er...'

Peter snapped. 'Just tell us will you.'

George could tell that whatever it was she knew she really didn't want to tell them. He wondered why.

'Alright, alright,' she said hesitantly. 'But it could be just a rumour – I mean it probably is. But I've heard that some Skullduffers, ones just like him are just big bullies.'

'So?'

'Well I've heard that they can't resist beating on people with greening, giving them serious injuries, that kind of thing.'

George was really confused. 'I don't understand. How's that going help?'

'Because of this,' said Molly. She pulled out a tissue from her pocket, then she spat on it, held it up to her face and started to rub. George noticed a tear in the corner of her eye.

Then George understood alright. Molly was removing her make-up, exposing the green skin beneath. Then he suddenly realised – the make-up – the anti-greening eye drops at the E. House. Molly had greening, and by the looks of it she had it bad – real bad.

Peter took a step back, 'Molz! I had no idea, you should have told me.'

'I didn't want anyone to know.'

George thought that he could understand why.

'Molz I'd never have been bragging about overwishing in front of you all the time if I'd have known about this. I'm so sorry.'

'It's OK Peter, really it is.' When she had finished wiping the make-up off she dropped her face to the ground.

Peter gently grabbed hold of her chin and raised her head. 'Molz it's nothing to be ashamed of, it's not your fault.'

'It's just embarrassing, that's all.'

'It's your mum and dad who should be embarrassed, not you,' he said angrily.

'Yeah I know but...'

'But nothing. It's their fault.' Visions of Molly's parents forcing her to overwish made George grow hot inside, and a vision of Mark leaning over the yellow bucket flashed through his mind. 'It's so their fault.'

'Anyway never mind that now,' said Molly. 'What I suppose I'm saying is that I could probably distract him.'

'No chance Molz, not in a million years,' said Peter putting his arm tightly about her. 'No way!'

'Well have you got any better ideas?'

Peter looked at George in a pleading kind of way. 'No but we'll think of something, really we will.'

The moments ticked by in silence.

And after a time it became obvious that none of them could think of a better idea.

'That's it, I've decided! I'm going to do it.' She shrugged Peter's arm from around her.

'I've already said no Molz, and I meant it.'

'Well I'm the only one here that can distract that Skullduffer, and if it gives you both a chance to find your mums then it's worth it.'

'You can't, you said he could give you *serious* injuries,' said George.

'I'll get over it. I can get fixed up at the hospital. That's it,' said Molly. 'I'm going.'

Peter grabbed her arm 'No you're not. Stay right there.'

'You can't stop me,' said Molly, punching his arm away from hers. 'I can do what I want.'

'Molz!'

But it was too late, Molly had stepped out into full view of the Skullduffer.

Peter stood there, aghast. George peered around the corner after her. He could see the Skullduffer eyeballing her. His mouth twitching, and his hands fidgeting. One of his grazed shoes began to tap on the ground.

'Oh no, it's going to work!' whispered George. 'Look he can't resist. Poor Molly.'

It was obvious that the Skullduffer was becoming agitated. The temptation to cause injury to Molly looked to be too much for him to bear. His foot began to tap harder – faster.

'He's going to go for it – any second now,' said George.

The Skullduffer looked from side to side. George bet he was checking to see that Joey was completely out of sight. He placed the golden cosh against the wall, put one fist inside the palm of his other hand, then cracked every knuckle of every finger.

Molly looked at him and away again quickly. She quickened her step.

Duffer Don followed her.

'Look,' said Peter. 'The idiot's left the cosh behind. If we can get that to Molz, she might be alright.'

Duffer Don caught up with her swiftly. He grabbed her shoulder, pulled her back towards him and tipped her upside down. The noise that followed was ear crunching – a loud crack. Molly let out a huge yelp, then she was dropped to the floor. George could see that her left leg had been snapped in two. She dragged herself along the floor, screaming in pain. Duffer Don raised his leg and sent it hurtling full force towards her side. George could see her arm dangling limply, just hanging there, right out of its socket.

Peter turned to face George. 'We've got to help her, and right now! Listen George, you go and get the gates open.' He handed the Master Key to him. 'I'll try and get the cosh to Molz. I'll meet you in there. If I'm not there in 15 minutes carry on without me.'

George didn't really like the idea of being left on his own.

Another scream – weaker this time. 'OK Peter. Good luck.'

They ran towards the gates. Peter snatched up the golden cosh and ran off towards Molly.

George took the Master Key out of the box. He looked at it, then at the lock. There was no way this key would open this lock, it was way too small. George heard the sound of a yelp – much deeper than before – a male – was it Peter? He pushed the key towards the lock, he could feel it growing in his hand, maybe it was going to work after all. He placed the key in the lock and turned it. Click. He pushed open the gates. Another yell. This time he could tell it wasn't Peter's or Molly's. George smiled, the bully was getting it back. An image of Stuart yelling in pain flashed through his mind, and made him smile even wider.

George stepped through the gates, and kept a lookout for Peter.

Several minutes later Peter came limping through the gate. George could see that he had a nasty bruise on his cheek.

'You OK?'

'Yeah, he clocked me a few blows, but then I used the cosh to break a few of his bones, then I gave it to Molz. I think she's going to be alright, but that Skullduffer's snivelling like a baby now, begging for mercy.'

'Good.'

'Come on then,' said Peter. 'Let's check this place out.'

They walked through a few trees towards Sir Augustine's house. It was ancient. Perched on the edge of a cliff, it was a gross fortress. They stood quietly in its shadow. George didn't know why – but he shuddered.

-Chapter Eleven-

THE RESCUE

Tall, black spires decorated the rooftops penetrating deep into the sky.

'Got a bad feeling, have you?' said Peter limping along.

'Yeah.'

'Come on let's get this over with.'

They used the Master Key to open the huge wooden door. George stared down the bleak corridor, he could feel the coldness off the grey walls prickling his skin. Peter walked over to the first door and pushed it open.

George's jaw dropped to the floor as he looked in. 'There must be millions worth of wishes here.' He felt a stirring in his stomach. 'I – I've never seen so much treasure.' George walked slowly around the room, emeralds, diamonds and rubies sparkled, gold blinging out from every corner. George could feel his eyes stretching to splitting point.

A gold and crystal grandfather clock in the corner chimed causing them to jump.

'How come he's got all this stuff and he's not dead?' asked George, picking up a diamond picture frame with a picture of Sir Augustine in it.

'No idea, this guy's loaded, he should be well dead by now.'

They went from room to room, each one filled to brimming point with riches. Then they came to a door that was locked.

Peter shook his head. 'I don't understand. Why would you lock this one and leave all the others unlocked? It doesn't make sense.'

'Unless there's *someone* in here,' said George quickly taking the key out of his pocket.

'Quick get it open.'

George turned the key and pushed open the door. It was dark inside.

'What the Helcrix is that?'

George could see a huge hall with lots of black tank-like boxes, the size of small cars. There was a blood-red light on the side of one of them. 'What's that light?'

Peter visibly trembled. '*That* doesn't look like a light to me, that looks like a container full of wish serum. Oh no! You don't think, you don't think that Sir Augustine's got someone in there do you?'

George somehow knew he wasn't going to like the answer to his next question. 'What do you mean?'

'Mum,' whispered Peter. 'What if my mum's in there. George you'll have to go and see, I can't look, honestly I can't.'

George didn't want to, but looking at Peter standing there so still and rigid, it didn't look like he really had a choice. He walked over. 'Peter I think they're tanks of some sort. They're full of water. *Oh no!*'

'What?'

There's...'

'What?'

'Well I'm not sure what they are, animals of some kind all dead, all just floating on top of the water like dead fish.'

Peter walked over.

'What are they?'

Peter took a staggered step back. 'They're Megaladoms, *baby* Megaladoms. Look at the needles in their necks. I know what's going on here. Sir Augustine's draining the wish serum from them so he can use it himself. And – oh no!'

'What?'

'You know how he owns the E. House, oh George I feel sick, I bet this is how we get all those free wishes.'

George suddenly felt a pang of guilt because he'd had free wishes from there too. He never would have even gone into the place if he'd known about this.

Peter pointed towards the blood-red light. 'Quick George, we need to get over to that one, it might not be too late.'

They ran over. George stared in at the limp, pale green, dragon-like creature, not quite floating on the top, but not far off. 'Do you think we can save it?'

'We need to get it back to the sea, that's its only chance!'

'Let's get this tank open.'

'Just there,' said Peter reaching past George, grabbing a handle and pulling at it. The lid began to lift up. 'I'll hold this open George, if you can reach in and get to it.'

George plunged his arm into the ice-cold water and felt about for the Megaladom. 'Got it,' he said clasping his hand around the leathery body.

Peter thrust his hand into the tank. 'Let me take the needle out, while it's still underwater.' 'That's it!' George felt the Megaladom jerk back in his hand. 'Right. Now how do we get it to the sea?'

Let's try those doors,' said Peter. He went over and opened them up. George felt a blast of icy air surge on him.

'George, there's a balcony here on the cliff, but it's a bit of a tricky climb down to the sea. 'Sorry George but I don't think there's any way I'll make it, my leg's too sore.'

'Its OK I'll do it,' said George.

'You'll have to be quick George, Megaladoms can't last long out of the water.'

'Right.' George hauled the creature out of the tank as gently and as quickly as he could. He placed it inside his jacket. He could feel the Megaladom's claws trying to grip onto his chest and he could already hear it gasping for water.

'You sure you're going to be OK?'

'Hope so.'

'Be careful!'

George stepped out onto the balcony. Sea spray whipped across his face, and he quivered all the way down to his toes. He looked down. The wind was beating the waves silver – curling them up into the black night air – smashing, exploding them onto the jagged rocks down below. He hesitated for a second – but he knew that he had to go – and now, if this Megaladom was to stand any chance of survival.

He climbed up onto the balcony wall, and lowered his shivering body onto the rock face. The deafening applause of the sea surrounded him, and the wind tried hard to take his grip. But George was determined. The spiky rocks ripped at his hands, and tore at his legs, but still he carried on, descending, step by treacherous step down towards the black hostile sea.

Eventually George dared himself to look down. Nearly there now, just one last step, that should do it. He heaved himself down onto a narrow ledge, waves snatching and snarling at him. He grabbed onto a jutting rock with one hand and with the other he opened up his jacket and took hold of the now lifeless Megaladom.

'*Come on,*' he screamed at the sea. 'Come to me. Time's running out.'

He waited for the next wave to come to him. Here it was, coming now. He was ready. He leaned towards the wave as it rose up towards him. He tightened his grip on the rock and held out his arm. The wave smashed over the lower half of his body, and George let go of the Megaladom. He watched as the sea took it away – then something – yes. He was sure there had been a movement.

George turned to face the cliff: now the hard part. He looked up into the nightness. He needed to get a move on. He hoped Peter had waited for him. He took in a deep but spikingly cold breath. He lifted up his leg.

From way above, George heard the faint sound of someone screaming.

-Chapter Twelve-

THE GREAT WHITE SAPPHIRE

There came the sound of a roar fast approaching. Quickly George turned around. The sea was bubbling – regurgitating – spewing something. Something was down there – *and something was moving towards him.* He watched as the sea began to split in two. Something was rising up, he could tell it was huge, water gushing off its sides. And then, a tidal wave of water falling from its heights, crashing back into the sea.

And there it was. A huge white jewel. As big as a castle. George had never seen anything so terrifying – so awesome. Then he realised what it must be – what it was – the Great White Sapphire. But there was something else.

A savage wave, like a monstrous open mouth coming towards him. He couldn't move – *there was nowhere to move.* The chill of the sea enclosed on him, swallowed him, dragged him towards its bottom – towards its emptiness. A bubbling thud of echoes surrounded him. Creepy ribbons of slimy seaweed searching – searching to contain him – like a mass of black tentacles. The undercurrent twisted and writhed his body until he could feel himself crushing beneath its purpose. And still further down he went, salt grating his eyes and burning his skin. Iciness shrinking his innards. With all his strength George battered his legs, and struggled his arms against the invisible force. He was going to die.

But wait – what was that? A light, he could see a light. What was it? Oh my God – it was a window – a window under the sea – in the Great White Sapphire – and a room on the other side. He was heading towards it. The sea was taking him there. He dragged his limbs through the water – he might make it. There was *someone* there, someone in the room. He could bang on the window, they might see him. Maybe they could help. He reached out. He grasped onto a jagged sapphire rock and pulled himself towards the window. He pounded his fists against the windowpane – soundless – muffled – nothing. He watched as the person, a woman he thought, walked away towards the far side of the room. He pummelled the window, silently screaming for help with his eyes. He glared in as he watched her leave the room, turning the light off behind her. Darkness.

Tension soared through his body, and his lungs raged with fire as his heart became cold. Then panic invaded his thoughts, and visions of death tore at his brain until he could almost feel it bleed.

Come on – he screamed within – *you have to fight harder than this.*

He grappled about in the bleakness for another sapphire rock. He found one. He pulled himself upwards.

That's it, and another.

He found another. Upwards again, until eventually he could see broken ripples of moonlight skimming the surface, and for a moment he thought he might make it. But the sea was pitiless and his clothes heavy. Progress was slow, way too slow.

Come on – he whispered, *time's running out.*

He needed air – tiring – failing now. His lips began to part, water began to trickle into his mouth. Blackness slowly crept over his eyes. His body became rigid. No escape now. This was his end. He was going to have to breathe.

GASP!

His head sliced through the surface of the sea. He spluttered as the air – icy, brisk, soothing air entered his fiery lungs. The screeching wind pierced through his eardrums. Rain – wonderful storm-like rain stinging him like acid whips. He breathed another starving breath, and another. He opened his eyes and looked up at the Great White Sapphire – silver raindrops rushed toward him.

Maybe he could climb it. Did he have the energy? He had no choice, he had to get out of the sea, and soon, because he could feel its coldness killing him.

Taking in one massive breath George heaved his pathetic body out of the sea, the greedy wind attempting to drag him away – but George gripped hard. The rocks shredded at his already torn hands, and George saw his blood staining the rainwater pink. Upwards he went, towards the dimly lit sky. He looked down. If he was to lose his footing now, he would be sure to die. Almost as soon as George had thought this then the wind took one of his feet from under him. He was going to lose his grip – he was going to fall. His wet clothes pulling – dragging him down. He searched for another footing with his dangling leg, his hands slipping away from the rocks.

No – can't fall – not now – *will die – will die* – find a rock – *come on.*

Just in time his quivering foot found a large protruding sapphire. 'Phew! That was close.'

He remained still for a moment to try to get his breath back, his heart feeling like it was pumping glue. He looked up. Just one last push.

'*Yes Yes Yes!*' he yelled when he reached the top. His body quivered in the wind, and though the water was draining from him he still felt as though he was drowning. He gasped for air again, still disbelieving that he could. He collapsed onto the small surface, he could wait here until someone saved him.

Surely Peter would have alerted someone by now. He looked out to sea to catch any sight of a boat. No sign yet. But hang on a minute, there was something in the sky, what was it – a helicopter maybe? Whatever it was, was heading towards him and at great speed, no lights on. Oh no, it wasn't a helicopter, he could see it now, it was a Megaladom, a huge Megaladom. There was nowhere to hide and it was coming right for him. He pulled his knees to his chest, lowered his head and braced himself in anticipation of being snatched up by its claws. But the pick up didn't happen. He waited, listened, he could just hear the sound of wings flapping, and the lashing rain beating on something leathery. He turned his head slowly upwards. The Megaladom was hovering above him, what was it doing? A screech like a dinosaur's, right up into the night air, contented almost, and then another. Then it folded up its wings and dived into the sea.

George shook his head in disbelief. Was that a thank you? No, surely not. He shifted himself onto his knees to peer over the side to check it had definitely gone.

'Ouch!' What was that, something hard had caught his knee? He stood up. A round handle, like the ones they have in submarines. That could only mean a door. George stared down at it, what should he do? He should try and open it, if he could get inside he could get warm, it might be his only chance, other than a freezing death. And what if *he* was the one to rescue Mrs Hubbins, he would be a hero. No one back home would ever believe it of him – not him, George, he certainly wasn't the likeliest of heroes. But hey, maybe he should give it a go.

He bent down, clutched the handle with both hands and turned it, easily. With every turn of the handle a whole section of the top of the Great White Sapphire moved over, until enough had repositioned for George to look down inside. He couldn't see anything; there was nothing to see. Just a huge drop, and way, way down below a yellow doorway. He looked back up, towards the sky and down to the sea. His brain was filled with one thought – *cold – cold – cold*. George stared back down into the chasm, wanting its warmth and protection. George leaned right over, his clothes wringing themselves out on the edge. But wait – the water wasn't falling all the way to the bottom, it was settling just a short distance from him, forming a puddle, right there just below him.

A glass floor? It must be. If it was, it could be his chance, his only chance to get out of this cold. George opened the entrance a little wider, enough for him to squeeze right through. He lowered himself down by his arms through the narrow gap. He felt for the glass floor beneath his tiptoes. There it was, he could feel it, there was definitely something there. Was he brave enough to let go? If he let go and it wasn't a floor then he would fall all the way to the bottom. It wasn't an easy decision, fall or freeze to death?

But his body was making the decision for him, and he felt his hands losing their grip, as slowly, very slowly they slipped away.

George dropped from his tiptoes – to the flat of his foot. There *was* something there, holding him up. He *was* standing on something.

'Yes, yes, yes!'

Slightly warmer already.

He looked down, his head jolted backwards. It wasn't glass – it was nothing! He looked down again, this time very slowly. He was definitely standing on nothing. He shuffled his feet about and went to take a step forwards, but just as he feared there wasn't anything there – just space, nothing else. He could feel his whole body shake. For a moment George considered going back outside, but it was so much more sheltered in here, and he didn't really think he could reach anyway. Yes he needed to stay here – he was less likely to freeze to death. Maybe he could just stand there until someone came to his rescue, but that could take days – weeks – never. But what else could he do? His only hope was to find a way to the bottom, but how could he do that?

George stood still, stiller than he had ever stood in his life. And then a thought, a sudden crazy thought. What if it *was* something he was standing on and he just couldn't see it. Maybe there was one thing he could try – no – it couldn't be – could it?

George quickly unzipped his pocket, and pulled out the box containing the invisible torch. The box was soaking wet and fell apart in his fingers. George watched it drop down to the floor below; it took several seconds to land. George tightened his grip on the torch. He flicked the switch. He directed the torch downwards to where his feet were.

'*Wicked!*'

He could see a circle of red carpet, he waved the torch about, it was a step – and there was another – and another. He lowered his left foot onto the invisible step. It was solid.

'Awesome!' He checked for a banister. There was a wooden one over to his left side. He grabbed hold of it.

George gradually made his way down to the bottom until the yellow door was before him. He took hold of the door handle. He didn't know what to expect. Whoever was in there had unimaginable powers, though George knew he had some pretty impressive ones of his own. He prayed that it wasn't his mum behind these doors, and that she wasn't the one responsible for all of this. He took in one slow, huge breath. He turned the handle and slowly, quietly opened the door. He glanced around the door into a library; there was no one there. He stepped inside. There was no tied up body – or dead body, as he had been kind of expecting. He made his way to the only other door in the room, he could hear voices. He tiptoed over and pressed his ear up against the door. Muffled voices; he couldn't make out what they were saying. He quietly opened the door.

-Chapter Thirteen-

THE BATTLE OF WISHES

'Yes dear, but how long are we going to stay here? Can't we move soon, I'm getting a little nervous? It's all very well showing off, but what if someone finds us in here?'

'We've locked the front door and there's no other way in,' came the voice of a man from the far end of the room. 'But you're right, we should probably move soon. I suppose I just wanted to show off our power for a bit.'

'I know dear, but I'd rather be some place more comfortable. I mean we can't even step outside without getting soaking wet.'

Oh no – it couldn't be – that was Mrs Hubbins' voice. What was going on? George pushed on the door to open it a tiny bit more. He pressed his eye up to the gap. He could see a man – a man he recognised. He'd seen enough pictures and posters of him all over Leesome Shrouds – Sir Augustine. George watched as he walked over to Mrs Hubbins, and put his arm around her. 'You can have whatever you want now, you know that. We shall leave tomorrow.'

George decided he'd heard enough. He pushed open the door.

'What's going on?' he shouted.

Mrs Hubbins and Sir Augustine jumped.

'Who the Helcrix are you?' demanded Sir Augustine walking up to him.

'George!' shouted Mrs Hubbins her voice shaking. 'What are you doing here?'

'I've come to rescue *you*!'

'Rescue me?' she said awkwardly. 'Why?'

'Why?' said George. 'What do you mean – why? You've been kidnapped.'

'I've been no such thing!'

'Will someone tell me what's going on?' shouted George.

'Well it's a long story dear.'

'Don't dear me,' said George, shivering and dripping water all over the floor. 'And – well I've got plenty of time. After all I'm stuck in a rock in the middle of the sea.'

'There's no need to be like that George,' said Mrs Hubbins.

He shouted. 'There's every need. I nearly died twice trying to get here.'

'I think that's probably a bit of an exaggeration,' snapped Sir Augustine.

'It is not!' yelled George. 'Anyway never mind that. What's going on? It's you isn't it – both of you – you're the ones that have the Crux?'

'Well,' said Mrs Hubbins hesitating, 'Yes we do have it George, *but* we didn't destroy the Blood Ghost. Sir Augustine rescued it so that we can do good with it.'

'But why you *two*?' asked George.

'Well when Anne came to see *me*, to tell me her worries about some information she had uncovered about *a man* that had plans to take the Crux, there was... an attraction,' said Sir Augustine. 'You see George there are some things you just can't help but give into. *Greed* is one – oh, and – yes, I suppose, love, is another.'

'Poor Mr Hubbins,' said George. 'He's going to be gutted!'

'How is he? Did he get my letter?' said Mrs Hubbins. 'You know I never meant to hurt him, I just...'

'What letter?' said George.

'The letter I left in my office.'

'There wasn't a letter,' said George shaking his head. 'Just Edwin Brown. I suppose killing him was all part of your plan too?'

'What do you mean?' asked Mrs Hubbins. 'What's happened to dear Edwin?'

'He was twisted to death,' said George. 'And he was wished that way – and – oh – there wasn't a body – and, well it's all a bit of a mystery.'

A look of horror swept over her face. '*Oh no*. That's terrible. When was this?'

'Well, I'd had a right shock in the Tunnel of Trances so Peter said that you'd know what to do. When we got to your office we found it ransacked and Edwin Brown was there – all twisted – twisted to death. It was disgusting.'

'Oh how awful.' Mrs Hubbins covered her mouth with her hand. 'Why would anyone do something like that, and why was my office ransacked?'

'I don't know. So it wasn't you two?' said George.

'No. It certainly was not!' shouted Mrs Hubbins.

'Then who was it?'

She said. 'I don't know!' Then she tilted her head for a moment. 'But – well – at least it wasn't *me*. Unless –' She turned around to face Sir Augustine. 'Augustine?' she said slowly.

Sir Augustine stared back at her, narrowing his dark, sinister eyes.

Then, George could see it – black – black that reached all the way into his soul, and beyond. A shiver emerged from the core of George's body.

'It was *you*,' said George. 'You're the one – *you* killed Edwin Brown?'

'No!'

'Yes you did,' shouted George. 'I can see it. I can tell!'

'That man,' spat Sir Augustine. 'Nearly ruined everything. Caught me in Anne's office. Had come to warn her – about *me*. Discovered *my* plan.'

'What do you mean?' said Mrs Hubbins. 'What about you? What plan?'

'*I* splattered the Blood Ghost. *ME!*'

'But you told me someone else had done it, and that you'd rescued the Crux, to do good with. That we were going to save Leesome Shrouds.'

'Yes I said all that!'

'But,' said Mrs Hubbins, 'you couldn't have destroyed the Blood Ghost – you'd be dead too.'

'I did kill it!' shouted Sir Augustine. 'I'd planned it for years. Shot it with a slow release *Death Wish*. Gave me time to get the Crux. I watched it slowly turn from red to blue. I grabbed the Crux before it was completely destroyed, and then used it to protect myself. And as you can see my plan worked beautifully.'

Mrs Hubbins cried out. 'So it was you all along? And what about Edwin? Oh no! I don't know if I want to hear this.'

'*I'd* made a bit of a mess in your office and he threatened to report me. Report *ME*! I didn't like him – not one bit. He was a twisted little man, so *I* twisted him to death. He got just what he deserved!'

'OH NO!' cried Mrs Hubbins. 'Edwin was the kindest man there was, he didn't deserve that! What have *you* done? OH NO, what have I done? Augustine, you can't just go around killing people like that.'

'*I* can do anything *I* want now,' said Sir Augustine the corners of his mouth curling up. George had been right. 'Now *I* have the Crux.'

'This is just awful,' cried Mrs Hubbins. 'His poor family. *My* poor family. *What have I done?*'

'Forget about them,' shouted Sir Augustine. 'You're with *me* now!'

'What's happened to you?' cried Mrs Hubbins. 'You're not the person I thought you were. You showed me that you were – kind – caring – loving – *worth leaving my family for.*'

'But *I* am POWER now!' said Sir Augustine. 'That's why *I've* changed. *I* am ultimate power. Now *I* can be who *I* really want to be. Who *I* am. Who I've always wanted to be.'

'I need a drink!' said Mrs Hubbins as she marched over to a drinks cabinet and poured herself a huge glass of something strong looking. George could hear the ice in the glass rattling on the sides. She drank it all, slammed it down and collapsed herself down onto a chair. She sighed as she put her head into her hands. 'So you didn't want the Crux to protect it from evil, and do good like you said you did. You wanted it for yourself.'

'Of course *I* did,' said Sir Augustine, his cold eyes staring. 'But I'm prepared to share it with you Anne. Just think, you can have whatever you want, wouldn't you like that? Course you would, that's what everyone wants.'

'Augustine,' she cried. 'I wanted to be with you because I thought you stood for all things good. Now – well now, you're just a – *a murderer.* I've made a terrible mistake.'

'Have it your way,' said Sir Augustine, not seeming overly bothered. He walked over to a picture of himself on the wall. He moved it to the side; there was a safe behind it. He opened it up, reached inside and took hold of something. George could see a glint of something metallic in his tightly clenched hand. George supposed it was the Crux. But what did Sir Augustine need that for? What was he going to do? Was he going to kill them?

'Maybe it's time I was leaving,' said George, not really having a clue how he would do that.

'I'll be the decider of that,' shouted Sir Augustine. 'But first we need to clear up a few things.'

'What?' said George.

'If you promise to keep this whole thing quiet, there will be no severe repercussions,' said Sir Augustine.

'But I have to tell my friends,' mumbled George. 'I can't keep this a secret. They need to know about their mum.'

'Then I can't let you go. I shall have to kill you!' shouted Sir Augustine.

'No Augustine, please no! Don't talk like this,' said Mrs Hubbins suddenly jumping up from the chair. 'George won't tell anyone, will you George?'

'Maybe just a little pain then. Just to ensure you don't tell tales! The kind of pain you won't forget in a hurry. The kind of pain you won't want to experience again.'

'No!' begged George. '*Please!* I've had enough pain today to last a lifetime, please I couldn't stand any more.'

Sir Augustine raised his hand.

'NO!' shouted Mrs Hubbins jumping in front of George. 'George tell him you won't tell them.'

'I won't, I won't tell them. I promise!'

Sir Augustine lowered his arm slightly, George breathed out a little. Now the crazed Sir Augustine began pacing up and down the room. Then he thought out loud that he should throw George back into the sea. George knew that he would never survive another spell out there, and so began to suggest alternatives. 'Maybe a helicopter, a boat even, either would do.'

'Trying to be smart, eh?' shouted Sir Augustine. 'Well let's see just how smart you are?'

Sir Augustine raised his arm again, and muttered something under his breath. George felt an incredible sharp pain take his legs from under him. He fell with a loud crash to the floor.

'What did you do that for?' yelled George, clutching his thigh as he scrambled to his feet.

'Because you're irritating *me*. That's why.'

No sooner had George stood up than he felt a massive blow to his stomach. The dull, sharpness of the blow resonated up to his chest, he gasped for the tiniest bit of breath.

'Augustine,' yelled Mrs Hubbins. 'No! Stop! Please.'

Images of fights with Stuart and his gang after school sliced through George's mind. He felt sick, he just hated fighting, probably because he wasn't particularly good at it. And this Sir Augustine was a lunatic – beyond mad. He was laughing a deep, wicked laugh now – he was actually enjoying this. He raised his arm again.

George quickly ducked behind the armchair. He could hear Sir Augustine laughing even louder. 'You think that hiding behind a chair is going to save you?'

'Augustine! No,' shouted Mrs Hubbins.

George could hear a struggle. Then he felt a thump as Mrs Hubbins' body collapsed into a jumble at his side. She grasped his arm.

'George – *I'm sorry.* Sorry to *you*, sorry to everyone. George if I don't get to see my family again – will you tell them – will you tell them, that I'm truly sorry, and that I love them – *both* of them – and Molly and Mark too – and that I made a terrible mistake.'

'That's if I ever get out of here alive. Look there's something I need to ask you.'

'George wait,' said Mrs Hubbins squeezing his arm tighter. 'Listen to me. There's something I need to tell you – this is important. Your mum, I think she's in Leesome Shrouds. A woman, I remembered her, she looked just like you. I worked with her years ago. I made an appointment to see her, but I didn't make it. She doesn't know about you George. But it all makes sense.'

'Enough! Enough of this sentimental rubbish!' shouted Sir Augustine his voice getting closer.

Mrs Hubbins pressed her mouth up against George's ear. 'She runs the orphanage – St George's Orphanage.'

George felt his heart stop – dead – was *this* for real? Was Mrs Hubbins telling him the truth? Was it possible that his mum really was alive? That was it, he had to get out. He had to do something – something to stop Sir Augustine from killing him. He had to find out if his mum was alive. But what could he do now? Too many thoughts, all at once.

George saw a pair of expensive brown leather shoes by his side and he looked up. Sir Augustine was leering down at him.

Hurry, time was running out – he had to think – and he had to be quick. That was it, he'd got it. George stood tall from behind the chair.

'Sir Augustine laughed loudly – a laugh so cruel it made the hairs on George's arms stand upright.

'So you think you can take *me* on – *me?*'

'Whatever you wish on me,' shouted George, 'I wish it back on you – only twice as hard.'

'You stupid boy,' said Sir Augustine laughing. 'You'll be sick from overwishing in no time. This is going to be easy.'

George felt his feet being lifted off the ground – he was flying through the air – CRASH! His body collided with immense force against the wall. He lifted up his head just in time to see Sir Augustine being propelled through the air towards the opposite wall – quicker – faster than George had been. The noise crashed through George's ears. Sir Augustine picked himself up, shaking his head.

'You'll be sorry for that,' he roared, and lifted up his hand once again.

George's head was walloped sideways, causing him to plough into a bookcase. The pain from his temple screeched through his brain. He could feel fluid dripping down his cheek – was it blood?

There was a crack from the other side of the room. George looked up to see Sir Augustine on his knees, trying to stand up.

'One more should do it,' said Sir Augustine breathlessly. 'Then you'll be too sick to defend yourself.'

George felt a great force raise him up from the floor, way too fast. He crashed into the ceiling, and then into the wall and down onto the floor. He struggled to catch his breath as he untangled his battered limbs from his heap.

Then there was a horrific smash, the sound of glass. George looked over. Sir Augustine was lying in a pile of broken glass; he had collided with the drinks trolley. He lay on the floor, lacerated – blood spilling from him. He didn't even attempt to get up. Glaring at George he said quietly, 'I will...kill you...' and he closed his rolling eyes. His hand went limp – something rolled out onto the floor. George watched as Mrs Hubbins' hand snatched it up.

'You'll be alright now...' came the fading voice of Mrs Hubbins.

Who was she talking to? Him? Sir Augustine? Herself? He tried to look up at her face, but his head became heavy, so heavy he couldn't lift it up. What was happening now? His eyelids weighed down – closing. *No* – must keep them open – Sir Augustine – will kill me.

But George couldn't help it. He closed his eyes.

-Chapter Fourteen-

THE AWAKENING

George could hear voices, familiar voices – far away. Dreaming – must be dreaming. *Who's there? Can hear now, voices getting clearer. Who is it? Can't open eyes – stuck together.*

'I'm sure I saw his hand move,' said a muffled voice.

Another voice now. 'You keep saying that.'

'What will we do if he doesn't wake up?' A girl's voice.

A boy's voice. 'I suppose we'll have to dispose of his body in the...'

'Peter stop! You can't say things like that!'

'LOOK. Look there, at his hands, they're moving. I told you they'd moved.'

'George, George, wake up.'

A hand gently rocking his body. He could feel his eyelids now – *come on – open.* That's it – but blurred images – a face. Who?

'Oh George!'

George recognised the voice, but who was it? He knew it. That's it. *Molly* – yes it was Molly's voice. That meant he was still in Leesome Shrouds. He opened his eyes – hazy, he blinked, and blinked again – images getting clearer now. Focus. Someone – *no* – more than one – leaning over him. Molly and Peter all smiling. Molly was head to foot in plaster.

'Hi,' said George attempting a smile. He looked around: he was in Peter's room.

Molly was crying now. 'Oh George, we thought you'd never wake up.'

Peter smiled. 'How are you feeling George? Are you OK?'

'Yeah, I suppose.' He tried to slowly sit up in bed. 'Just feeling a bit stiff that's all, and a bit groggy.'

'I'm not surprised,' said Molly. 'You've been asleep for ten days.'

'You're joking?'

'No, Mum must have put some sort of wish on you to make you sleep for ages.'

'But why? Why would your mum do that?'

'Can't you remember?' asked Molly.

'What?' asked George.

'Anything.'

George couldn't think, couldn't remember. What could he remember? That's it – the fortress. He shivered. Sir Augustine's treasures. The Megaladom, drowning in air. Great White Sapphire – invisible stairs – then what? Think. George closed his eyes tightly. Hang on – Mrs Hubbins and Sir Augustine *together*.

'I remember now Sir Augustine – he was the one. He twisted Edwin Brown to death.'

'Yeah and Mum helped him.'

Then George suddenly remembered the look of horror on Mrs Hubbins' face when she had found out that Sir Augustine was responsible for the death of her good friend Edwin Brown. 'Peter, your mum didn't know anything about it.'

'Really?' said Peter. 'I didn't know that. Well I suppose that makes things a bit better.'

George shuffled further up the bed. 'And I remember, your mum thought that they had *rescued* the Crux – to keep it safe – to do good things.'

'Did she?' said Peter. 'Really?'

'Yeah. And she told me to tell you all that she loves you. *OH NO!*'

'What?'

'A fight. I had a fight with Sir Augustine.'

Molly nodded. 'That makes sense – you were covered in bruises when we found you on the doorstep.'

'On the doorstep? Classy!'

'Can you remember anything else?' asked Peter.

'I remember him beating me up. I had to think of something. So I wished that every wish he wished on me he would get it back twice as hard.'

'Nice one,' said Peter.

George winced. 'Pain, I remember, worst pain ever. And then, oh no, Sir Augustine. I THINK I KILLED HIM.'

'You what?' said Molly, not looking half as horrified as George would have expected.

'He landed on the drinks cabinet. Glass everywhere, *blood,* glass.'

'Good riddance,' said Peter. 'If I were you I'd try not to think about it too much. Just forget about it George, honestly. After what he's done no one will be bothered if he's dead.'

But George couldn't forget– the memories piercing his brain like 1,000 fibre-optic needles. But there was more, he knew there was more – he just needed to remember – but the vision of the bloody Sir Augustine wouldn't shift out from his thoughts. George felt a cold shudder surge right through him. 'Sir Augustine's eyes. I watched them – they rolled round in his head – that's when I think he died. *The Crux* – it fell – it fell out of his hand.' He turned to look at Peter. 'Your mum – *she has the Crux.*'

'I know.'

George's eyes were wide open. 'MY MUM!'

'George – what is it?'

'Your mum – she said *my mum* was here – here in Leesome shrouds. They were supposed to meet – but they didn't. Oh my God – that's it – St George's Orphanage. George swung his heavy legs out of the bed. 'That's where she is. There's a place called St George's Orphanage in Leesome Shrouds right?'

'Yeah,' said Molly. 'There is but...'

'I have to go there. Where is it? Tell me where it is! I have to go there – *now!*'

'We'll come with you,' said Peter.

'No,' said George holding onto the wall for support. 'I need to do this on my own. Just tell me where it is.'

'It's right behind the Banishing Block,' said Molly. 'You can't miss it – it's the only white building in Leesome Shrouds.'

'I remember it. It was the first building I saw when I got here. Oh no, just think, if I'd have knocked there, then all of this might not have happened.'

'Are you sure you don't want us to come with you?' said Molly. 'You're really weak.'

'I'll be fine,' replied George, staggering out of the door. 'I think I'm going to be just fine.'

-Chapter Fifteen-

ST GEORGE'S ORPHANAGE

George stared up at the white building and over towards the red door. He could hear children playing. Why had Mum chosen all these children over him, it just wasn't fair? Maybe she just didn't want him. What if she didn't want to know him now? What if she slammed the door in his face? What if she *hated* him? He should go now – leave and not come back – ever. He turned to run, and caught sight of the Banishing Block. Strange, from this angle it looked vaguely familiar. A vision of an old man flashed into his mind, an old man sitting on a chair outside, a blanket tucked tightly around his legs. A pale man, grey hair, he was thin, really thin. The flesh of his cheeks recessed deep into his skull. He wasn't moving. George remembered looking up at Mum, she looked sad, real sad.

George shivered, was drawn back to his present situation. He turned back around to face the door.

You can't leave now – you have to do this – you have to find out if it's her, once and for all.

But George couldn't move – his body saturated in fear, and a hope so huge that it paralysed him. After several minutes had passed, he grabbed hold of the handrail and forced his trembling legs to carry him up the couple of steps to the front door. He raised his hand to knock, but immediately pulled it straight back down by his side. It was no good, he couldn't do it; he turned to leave.

STOP! What was he thinking – he had to do it. Of course he had to do it, and now, right this second!

He reached up and knocked hard, feeling his body tense up as he did so. He bent his head and stared down at the WELCOME doormat. He could hear footsteps approaching. He should run – *now*. But it was too late, the door was opening.

'Hello,' came a woman's voice. 'Can I help you?'

George stared at the woman's dull grey shoes, not daring to raise his gaze.

'Are you alright?' asked the woman, reaching out and softly touching his arm.

'Yeah,' said George, slowly lifting his head to face her. There, he was doing it. He was going to look at her. *But* his heart stabbed him. There she was – this woman – a stranger – *not* his mum.

'Are you sure you're OK?' she said, withdrawing her head slightly. 'You're awfully white.'

'Yeah – I'm OK,' said George. 'I was just hoping, well, hoping that you were someone else.'

The woman smiled. 'Who was it you were looking for?'

'Mrs Price,' said George. 'Mrs Louisa Price.'

'I'll go and get her, shall I? Who shall I say's calling?'

Another chance, he had another chance.

'George,' he mumbled. 'Just say it's George.'

The woman pushed the door to, leaving it slightly ajar. George heard her walking away, he could hear voices – a gasp – then a moment's silence. Then he could hear someone running – someone running down the corridor – towards him. The door swung open.

'Mum!'

That face he had last seen in the Tunnel of Trances, exactly the same.

'George!' Mum gasped, raising a shaky hand to her open mouth and stumbling backwards. 'Oh George. Is it really you?'

'Yeah,' was all he could think to say.

'I can't believe it!' she said, tears dampening her white collar. 'I thought I'd never see you again. Look at you – oh my, how you've grown. You're so tall – so handsome.'

George said nothing, he didn't know what to say.

'How did you find me?'

His voice broke. 'Mrs Hubbins told me where you were.'

'I had an appointment with her but she didn't show up,' Mum said. 'I wondered what she wanted. I worked with her years ago for a short time but I hadn't heard from her since. She told me she had something important to tell me, but I never guessed it was something like this. And this was it – *you. Oh come here.*' She hugged him to her.

Lingering memories of his childhood shifted in his mind, and a peculiar sadness, an emptiness sprawled right through him. His shoulders were shuddering now – he felt like he was choking – choking on the swelling in his throat. Heart going too fast. Mum pulled him in even tighter – he couldn't breath, he was suffocating. He pulled away from her unfamiliar clutches. He looked at the damp patch his tears had left on the shoulder of her dress. He gasped for air – *there was no air* – he gasped again – and again – still no air – feeling dizzy now – everything whizzing. He felt an arm around his waist.

'Come on. Let's get you inside.'

George struggled along the corridor. He could hear the beeping of hospital machines, and a wheelchair looked abandoned outside one of the doors. The hazy outline of a young boy ran by him.

'*Walk* Jonathon!' Mum said in a stern voice.

Why hadn't Mum been at home to tell him off like that – like a real mum was supposed to – instead of doing it with these other children – these strangers? Mums were supposed to care about their own children – not someone else's.

She took him into an office. George heard the door close behind them.

She guided him over to a large sofa. 'Darling, come and sit down. It's all been a bit of a shock, hasn't it?'

'Yeah,' gasped George.

'Just take long, deep breaths. Nice and slow.'

George did as she said, and after a time began to feel less deathly.

'That's it.' Mum poured him some water from a jug on the side. 'Any better?'

'Yeah,' he said, sipping some of it. 'Sorry about that, don't know what happened.'

'You've nothing to be sorry about, nothing at all.' She sat beside him and began to gently stroke his back. 'It was just a bit of a panic attack, that's all. You'll be OK in a minute.'

George wiped the moisture from his cheeks.

'Oh George we've got so much to catch up on I don't know where to start. And I've got so much to explain to you.'

'Yeah,' said George, glancing around the room at all the photographs of other children – none of *him*. 'You have.'

'How's your dad?'

'He's OK I suppose,' said George remembering the bouts of depression. Wonders why you left us.'

'Darling, I didn't leave you,' said Mum. 'I promise I didn't leave you. I...'

'Then why didn't you come home?'

She shrugged her shoulders. 'Because I'm trapped.'

'What do you mean – trapped? How?'

'I don't know. I just don't know. The lift just doesn't show up for me any more. For six years I've sat by the Banishing Block every time it was due – for days, nights, weeks – waiting and waiting just in case it would come. I came to the conclusion that the lift had just stopped being a portal. That it had just finished somehow – broke down maybe. That's why I thought I'd never see you again.'

'But now it's working again,' said George. 'Because it brought me here.'

'Oh why wasn't I there? I should have been there. I can't believe I missed it – in six years I've never missed it – just that one time.'

'Yeah,' said George, thinking that if she'd have been there he probably wouldn't be wanted for murder now. 'Why did you miss it?'

'We had an emergency,' said Mum. 'Reports had come in about a little girl – Caitlin – she'd collapsed. She desperately needed our help. I had to make a decision.'

George could feel an overwhelming feeling of jealousy sneak up inside him.

Stop it – it's not Caitlin's fault. You're being selfish.

'So I took my chance with her. See she's only ten years old, she was all alone, helpless. Lost her parents to overwishing when she was seven, so she'd been fending for herself ever since. She'd watched her mum and dad overwish all her life, so naturally she thought it was the right thing to do. When we found her she'd been overwishing so much she was unconscious – surrounded by all her wishes – hundreds of cuddly toys.'

Mum shook her head.

Stop it. Think about it – Caitlin hasn't got any parents, at least you had one, and you would have had two if Mum hadn't been trapped. You should be feeling sorry for this Caitlin, not jealous of her. Now stop it!

'See darling, her heart's so very small – so fragile – it's not been able to take the constant abuse. She's so very close to death. You understand, don't you George that I just had to help, to give her a chance. And there is a chance, a slight chance that we can save her.'

George tried to imagine – he imagined a little girl with long blonde hair and a pink dress, lying – dying on a pile of toys.

'Course,' he said.

'She just needed someone to help her,' said Mum.

George noticed her voice quivering. 'I think you made the right decision, I mean to stay and help her.'

'I've had to make some very hard decisions over these last two years,' said Mum. 'I was getting very sick, crying and obsessing about – well – you, your dad, the lift. I woke up one day and decided that I had to get on with my own life, the here and now. So I decided that I wanted to do something good, and I knew that I probably could because of my ability to wish without consequence. Do you know about that George?'

George nodded.

She smiled. 'So I decided that I wanted to help children, so that maybe I wouldn't feel so bad about neglecting my own child.'

'So *you* started the orphanage. There wasn't one here before that?'

'No there wasn't. I noticed that there were lots of children losing their parents to overwishing, being left with no one to care for them. So I set it up, and named it after the child I loved most in the universes.'

'St George's,' smiled George, swallowing so hard he was sure he could feel his brain shifting.

'Exactly,' said Mum. 'And it is a great place. We've helped hundreds of children.'

'I've got a friend you might be able to help. Molly, she's called.'

Mum leaned towards him. 'Tell me about her. I'd like to hear about all of your friends – all about you.'

'Well her mum and dad *make* her overwish. All the time.'

'Yes, unfortunately that kind of thing does go on quite a bit.' Mum was looking angry now. 'How anyone can do that to their own child? It's awful, just awful.'

'I know my friend Molly's got greening because she was buying anti-greening eye drops from the E. House, and when she took her make-up off her skin was like – well like – an alien head. And her brother, I saw him being sick too.'

Mum shook her head. 'The problem is the parents have more rights over their children than we have. So unfortunately there's nothing we can do, it's all very frustrating.'

'Oh,' said George, feeling disappointed. He had thought for a moment that she might have been able to help.

There was a light tapping on the door. Mum went over. George could hear a woman speaking.

'Sorry to disturb you Louisa – just to let you know, I'm off now. Miriam's got the keys to the medicine cabinet if you need them.'

'OK, thanks Janice,' said Mum glancing at her watch. 'I didn't realise it was that time already. How's Caitlin doing?'

'She's hanging in there,' said the woman. 'The doctor's given her 20mg of wish serum, hopefully that'll get her through the next 24 hours.'

'That's great news,' said Mum. 'Who's staying with her tonight?'

'Francis.'

'Oh that's good. Well goodnight then, Janice, and thanks. And thanks for everything. If I'm not in tomorrow, you'll keep everything ticking over, won't you – everything as it should be.'

'Oh – er – yes,' said Janice, sounding slightly bemused.

'OK. Bye then,' said Mum, closing the door and turning to George. 'It's almost eight o'clock, and we've got an early start in the morning.'

'Why?'

'The lift's due tomorrow,' said Mum smiling. 'Didn't you know?'

'No,' said George. 'So soon, I didn't realise. Probably because I've been asleep for ages.'

'I'm so excited,' she said. 'Just think, tomorrow we can go home. Me and you George, going home, all together at long last.'

'Awesome!' said George, trying to imagine his dad's face.

'Come on then,' said Mum. 'Let's go home.'

'You mean you don't live here at the orphanage?'

'No,' said Mum. '*We've* got a house in Green Park.'

'We?' said George.

'Me and you George.'

George smiled, but then thought of the last time he was at Green Park.

'But isn't everyone fighting there?'

'There was a bit of trouble there a week or two ago, but things seem to have calmed down now. Now everyone's found out that Sir Augustine was responsible and not the people with greening.'

'My friend Peter's going be so jealous when I tell him you've got a house there.'

'Your house too George, remember,' said Mum.

'Before we go to - er - *our* house,' said George. 'There's something I've got to do.'

'Oh yeah?' said Mum.

'I really need to go and see my friends, tell them what's happening. And I have to say goodbye because I won't have time tomorrow.'

'Course,' said Mum.

'I won't be long.'

'Alright,' said Mum. 'I'll wait here for you. I need to explain a few things to my work colleagues anyway, concoct a reason why I'm leaving so unexpectedly. But more importantly I need to say goodbye to the children.'

'OK Mum,' said George feeling bad that she was choosing *him* over all the sick and lonely children. I mean they needed her more than he did – didn't they? But then she was *his* mum, so she should be with him, right? Yes that was definitely right?

'You best get going then,' she said giving him a hug.

'I'll be as quick as I can.'

George ran through the streets of Leesome Shrouds, laughing loud, punching his fists into the air. He had just found his mum. This was one of the best days ever. Things were looking good. Now he knew he *was* loved. Now he was *rich*.

-Chapter Sixteen-

MARK'S WISHES

It wasn't long before George was knocking on the door of Umpteen Tib Lane for what he guessed would be the last time, on this visit to Leesome Shrouds anyway.

'Coming.'

George smiled – memories of his first day rushed about him.

Molly stood plasterless in the open doorway; she was wearing that orange dress again, the one she had been wearing when he met her. 'George, we've been worried sick, are you OK? Did you find her? Is everything alright? Come in.'

'Yeah, couldn't be better,' said George following Molly into the living room. Peter was watching a film on a huge 80 inch plasma screen.

'Peter look who's here.'

Peter turned round, reached for the remote and turned the sound down. 'George! How's it going?'

'Guess what, your mum was right, it was my mum. She's OK, she's just been trapped here, and she's not been able to get back home. For some reason the lift's not been showing up, been broken she reckons.'

'Oh George,' said Molly, looking like she was close to tears. 'That's great news. How are you feeling?'

'A bit shocked I suppose, I never thought I'd see here again.'

'Crazy eh?' said Peter.

'So now the lift's working again we're leaving tomorrow. Mum's coming back with me, so that's fantastic.'

'That's just brilliant George,' said Molly. 'Hey imagine your dad's face when he sees her.'

'I know. You should have seen mine when *I* did, I nearly died on the spot.'

Molly laughed. 'Bet you did. Can't begin to imagine...'

'Anyway, what's happened here, this place looks completely different. It's massive.'

'Mum's been making the house bigger and sending us all lots of presents,' said Peter. 'Great for me, but Dad's destroyed, he's hardly been out of his room since he found out and...'

Suddenly there was a loud, urgent almost, knock at the door. Peter ran over to see who it was. George could see Mark standing at the door with a massive grin on his face.

Molly rushed over to her brother. 'Is everything alright?'

'Better than alright,' replied Mark. 'I had to come round and tell you because this might affect you too, and you wouldn't even know about it. Oh hi, George, good to see you've woken up at last.'

'What might affect me?' said Molly frowning.

'Well, you know how Mum and Dad make us wish for things and then we get sick?'

'Course I do.'

Mark was grinning widely now. 'Well this last week, every time I've made a wish for them I've not been getting sick.'

'I don't understand?'

'*They have.*'

Molly shook her head. 'What do you mean? That doesn't make sense. I don't understand, how come?'

'I don't know. I've been thinking about it all week, and the only thing I can think of, is that now Aunty Anne has the Crux she's made it so that every time I make a wish it makes

133

them sick. How cool is that. Last night I got myself a brand new computer, a watch and a scooter, *and* they're all really good makes.'

Molly's hand shot up to her mouth. 'Mark!'

'No, it's OK. I'm fine. I don't feel one bit sick, but Mum and Dad are sharing the toilet at home to be sick in right this minute. I'll tell you what, I'm going to have some fun with this! There's loads of stuff I want. Oh and if any of you want anything just let me know.'

'Won't they be wondering why they're being sick though?' asked Molly.

'Yep,' said Mark puffing out his small chest. 'But even when they do find out, they'll never make me wish for anything else for them again will they, because they'll know that it'll make *them* ill, not me.'

'That's crazy!' said Peter. 'Do you think the Crux really has that much power?'

Molly was chewing on her lip, looking thoughtful. 'Must have. It just has to be Aunty Anne. I know it used to make her really angry when Mum and Dad would make us overwish. She was always having rows with them. It just has to be her. Who else could it be?'

'Anyway I'm off, just thought I best let you know,' said Mark heading towards the front door. 'I'm going round to Jake's, he wants a new set of drums.'

Molly gave him a big hug. 'Take it easy though Mark. I mean you don't know how long it's going to last for. It might not be permanent.'

'OK OK.' Mark skipped out of the door. 'See you.'

Molly shut the door behind him. 'You know I think I might just go up to my room, and see if there's anything I need. You know, just to check and see if I can do it too.'

134

'Hang on a minute, don't go just yet' said George. 'I haven't got long because I won't be staying here tonight, I'm going to stay at Mum's.'

'Oh, right,' said Molly. 'Course you are.'

'And I probably won't see you again after tonight, well not until the next lift comes anyway.'

Peter asked. 'Why not?'

'The lift leaves at seven in the morning, so I'll be going straight there from Mum's.'

Molly looked shocked. 'Oh!'

'So I've just popped round to say goodbye really.'

Molly and Peter said nothing.

'I should go up to my room and get a few bits.'

Molly dipped her head slowly. 'Yeah.'

'Talking of your room,' said Peter. 'We had a look in there when you were asleep, there's tonnes of stuff in there. How come?'

'I just wished for it,' said George grinning.

Peter's head shot up. *'No way!* If you'd have wished for that lot you'd have been sick as a Beazlefriar the whole time you were here.'

'Can you keep a secret?'

They both quickly nodded. George laughed.

'Well,' he said. 'I did find Stuart that day in the E. House.'

'But you said you didn't,' said Molly, a tinge of disappointment in her voice.

'I know what I said,' said George 'But I only said it because I had to. You see Stuart Crocker told me something that I couldn't tell you then, but I can now, because you're my friends and I trust you.'

'Go on,' said Peter impatiently.

'Because I'm not from Leesome Shrouds I can wish for whatever I want, without getting sick.'

'But you *were* sick, the day after you'd been to the E. House,' said Molly. 'And after that Libraria thing.'

'Only because of these.' George rifled through his pockets and showed them the sickness tablets.

George watched as his friends stared at the pills; then they stared at him and then they stared at him some more.

'I'll just go upstairs then, and pack.'

He walked silently up the stairs, listening for any signs that either of them had come out of shock. He fought his way into the bedroom. He looked around, moved some boxes off the bed and sat down. It wasn't going to be easy for him to leave. He'd become attached to this house, to Leesome Shrouds, and especially to his new friends. George swallowed back his distress. *Be strong – you can come back – you will come back –soon – one day.* He patted the bed affectionately and stood up.

There was a light tap on the door. Peter was there. 'You're so lucky you know. I'd give anything to be able to wish and not get sick, it's fantastic, honestly it is.'

'Yeah I know.'

'If I tell you a something George do you promise not to tell?'

'Yeah, course I won't.'

'I don't really like overwishing, never have,' said Peter. 'I just have to do it, you know in front of my mates, but I really hate the way it makes me feel.'

'Maybe they hate it too.'

'Maybe. But I guess I'll never find out. You just have to be seen to do it.'

George said nothing.

'The sickness is just so horrible.'

'I know.' George thought back to the sickness from the tablets.

Peter looked down at George's packed bag. 'So you ready to go?'

'Yeah, suppose. You know it's funny, I should be feeling great about seeing Dad again and Mum coming back but, well it's weird, now I feel kind of sad, sad about leaving, I think. Daft eh?'

Peter nodded. 'No, I know what you mean. Here, got you this, sort of a goodbye present.' He pulled a box out of his pocket. 'Just something that might come in handy back home.'

The package was scruffily wrapped.

George ripped the paper away.

Cheating Pens
Each pen answers five exams to grade A, seven to grade B or nine to grade C.
*Not suitable for mathematics.

'We can't use them here any more, the teachers know what they're looking for,' said Peter. 'But I thought you might be able to use them where you're from.'

'Thanks,' said George staring at the rather odd brown pens. Just think, he probably had enough here to see him through university, maybe he would be able to get a good job after all. The teachers had always said that he would struggle to make the grades, and to be honest he hadn't been that bothered, neither it appeared had his dad. He had just found it real hard to concentrate on anything for long, his mind wandering off all the time, creating all kinds of scenarios, ones of abandonment, betrayal, murder. But now Mum was alive, maybe he would be able to concentrate better in class, maybe now there was a chance that he might not need these pens at all.

'Think I best hide them from Mum and Dad though,' said George trying to remember the last time was he had used those two words in the same sentence. 'Don't think they'd approve.'

'Yeah, definitely.'

George sighed. 'Well I probably should get going, been quite an adventure eh?'

Peter grinned. 'You bet. Let's hope there's no more like that, don't think I could take it.'

'Know what you mean.'

Peter nodded into the bedroom. 'What you going to do with all that stuff?'

George pointed to his holdall. 'The journey in the lift's a bit rocky, don't think I could cope with any more stuff than this. You and Molly can have it.'

'You serious?'

George cast a glance back at all the wishes he had made. He thought back to when he had realised that he could wish for whatever he wanted consequence free. He smiled, it had been a night to remember alright. 'Yeah, course you can have it, who else would I give it to?'

'Wicked!'

George glanced at his watch. 'Right then...' He felt a large soft lump rise up in his throat.

'Time eh?'

George nodded.

'Come on then, let's get this over with.' George was sure he heard Peter's voice tremble.

Molly was waiting for them at the bottom of the stairs. George looked at her and Peter, much was changed. Over the last two weeks they'd shared so many experiences together, they'd become true friends and he knew he was going to miss them loads, and he also knew that there was a slight chance that they might never see each other again.

'You'll come back though won't you George?' said Molly sniffing loudly, the tears washing away some of her anti-greening make-up. 'Promise you will.'

He smiled at her. She really was quite pretty once you got your head past all that make-up. 'Course I will.'

She leapt over and gave him a long hug. He felt his cheeks blush and something flip over in his stomach. He stepped back. 'Well, I really hope so.' At that moment he felt something beyond sadness.

'You take it easy,' said Peter giving George a soft punch to his arm. 'And all that.'

George fought back tears; he had to leave, and right now. 'OK then, well I guess this is it. Well thanks for looking after me and – er – well – see you.' And he turned and walked out onto the misty lane.

Molly's voice followed him. 'Bye George. I'll miss you...'

He didn't look back.

-Chapter Seventeen-

GREEN PARK

'Is this it?' gasped George gazing up at the house his mum had pulled her convertible car outside.

'Yes.'

'It's massive,' he said. 'How many rooms does it have?'

'Thirty six,' said Mum, smiling at him. 'At the last count anyway.'

'Home's going to seem pretty small after living here.'

'I'd gladly have given all of this up just to spend another ten minutes with you and your dad. And I mean that darling.'

Mum opened the door, George staggered inside and slumped himself down onto a sofa. It allowed him to gawp up at the high ceilings and the tall walls. He sighed a deep sigh, took a deep breath in. Then he knew something.

'It was you?' said George. 'Of course it was you.'

'What darling? What was me?'

George could smell roses. 'The parcel, you put it in the lift for me.'

'Course I did, no one else could,' said Mum.

'But why?'

'Because I was going to show you the lift for your sixteenth birthday. I was hiding the presents there because I knew what a little snoop you were. If I'd have hidden them in the wardrobe you'd find them. I knew that you always found your Christmas presents well before Christmas.'

George felt his face redden.

'I was going to take you on a trip in the lift, and it would probably have been here, to Leesome Shrouds I mean, see if you remembered anything about being here before.'

'I've been here before?'

Mum looked sad now. 'Yes, when you were just five years old, I brought you to see your granddad.'

'My granddad lived in Leesome Shrouds?'

'Yes he did, for the last ten years of his life anyway. He loved it here.'

George could definitely understand why. 'You know, I think remember him.'

'Do you darling?'

'Yeah, I had a memory of him when I went to the Orphanage.'

'Yes he had a house there. That's why I built the Orphanage there.'

'He kind of looked like he was dead,' said George remembering the stillness.

'Well he wasn't, George, but he was very sick then and for a couple of years after. That's why I came over here that last time, because he was dying then.' A tear trembled in the corner of her eye. 'Then like I said, when it came time to come back the lift just didn't show.'

George said nothing.

Mum took in a very deep breath, shook her head. 'So then, did you open the parcel?'

George smiled at her. 'Course I did, it had my name on it, and it was a good job I did, I needed everything in it, especially that invisible torch.'

'Oh, said Mum, looking puzzled. 'How do you mean?'

'I needed it to get down some invisible stairs in the Great White Sapphire.'

'*Oh no,*' said Mum. 'Don't tell me that Interglobal Travellers have started bringing things from one world to another – that can only lead to disaster – *catastrophe* even.'

'What do you mean?'

She explained. 'That invisible torch was for Bleeding Rivers. You need it there because the place is littered with invisible things. You need a torch just so you won't fall over them and break your neck.'

'That's mad. How come everything's invisible?'

'Because Bleeding Rivers has an invisibility factory,' she said. 'Whatever you want making invisible they'll do it for you.'

'How?'

'By dipping it in a Top Secret Solution,' said Mum. 'I've heard the ingredients are all see through.'

'How do you mean?'

'Things like ground up glass, water, air, melted down diamonds. I've heard say that the secret ingredient is a drop of crystal clear, but no one really knows. To be honest with you the whole invisibility thing's a real nuisance. Some idiot even made an invisible car once – can you imagine that? Health and safety have got their work cut out over there, I tell you. But until invisibility gets banned then there's nothing anyone can do about it.'

'What are the other worlds like?'

'I'll tell you when we get home, when *you* tell me about those invisible stairs, and what you were doing in the Great White Sapphire,' said Mum smiling her beautiful smile at him. 'But for now, *bed* – remember we've got to be somewhere very special first thing in the morning!'

George lay in his new bed. It was warm and soft – just the way it should be – should have always been. He shivered with excitement, tomorrow was going to be the best day of his life. Mum was going home.

-Chapter Eighteen-

THE BANISHING BLOCK

George and his mum arrived at the Banishing Block, where he had arrived two weeks earlier. He looked at his watch; the lift was due any time now. They waited in silence. A familiar soft breeze swept across his face. This was it, he could feel it, he knew it was coming. He turned to look at his mum, she was staring at the wall. He followed her gaze. He watched as the stones began to shift in the wall, exposing the shabby little lift beneath.

'Great, it's here,' said George.

He turned to look at Mum and smiled – but something was wrong – he knew it.

'I can't!' she gasped, and turned to face him, her face white.

'What do you mean?' he said. 'Don't you want to come home?'

'YES,' she cried. 'Of course I do.'

'Then what?'

'*George*. I can't see it – I just can't see it. All I can see are stones. No lift, just stones.'

'*But it's there!*' cried George.

She sighed. 'No George. No, it's not there, not for me!'

'What?'

'It isn't there!'

'Please!' yelled George, thumping the wall several times. 'Don't do this. NO! This isn't fair, I've only just found you.'

'Darling don't,' said Mum, pulling him to her, 'you'll hurt yourself. Listen to me. It'll be OK – everything will be OK.'

'No it won't!' shouted George, pulling away from her. 'I'm not going. I'm going to stay here with you.'

'George you can't. Your dad needs to know the truth. You can come back to me, soon – very soon. The clocks go forward in six months – you can come and see me then. George look at me.'

He felt a warm hand gently lifting up his chin.

'George all you need to know is that I love you, and that I'm with you every minute of every day. And you never know, one day, *we* might figure out a way for me to get back home. But for now you have to be strong – you have to go!'

George shook his head. 'But what if I can't come back. What if the lift doesn't show for me, like it doesn't for you? I might never see you again.'

Mum was crying now. 'Darling, you'll be fine. You can't even think like that. You will be able to come back.'

George cried out. 'You don't know that for sure.'

'Darling, we *will* see each other again, even if I have to get the Crux to do it. And I mean that! George, are the doors open yet?'

For a moment George considered lying, but after a moment's thought he knew that would be the wrong thing to do. His mum was right, he did need to let Dad know about all of this.

'Yeah, they're open,' he said quietly, his throat choking him.

'You need to go,' she said, tears drenching her face. She grasped his hand in hers, and squeezed it tightly. 'Go, *now*. You have to go now. I love you George, so much.'

'Mum, I love you too.'

He turned to face the lift, unaware that he was still holding her hand.

'OK,' he said as he hurriedly took one massive step into the lift.

He felt a thud as his mum's hand left his, colliding with the stone wall on the other side. He turned around. The lift doors hadn't quite closed yet. He could see Mum. He knew she couldn't see him, but he could still see her through the closing gap. He could see her as she dropped to her knees. He could see her as she buried her face in her hands. He could see her whole body shaking. Then he could see her no more.

-Chapter Nineteen-

THE ARRIVAL

The lift doors opened. George could hear a train pulling out of the station. Eyes still shining with tears, he stepped out of the lift. Raising a trembling hand he erased the sweat from his forehead and the tears from his cheeks. He turned around, stared back into the lift and sighed. His magical mode of transport had given him some adventure alright, and he supposed that even though Mum was trapped, at least she was alive. He watched as the lift doors shut, and the wall enclose around it.

'See you next time,' he whispered.

He walked slowly along the platform. He could see a man on a nearby bench; he was holding his head in his hands. He was wearing a jacket that was familiar to him. He rushed over.

'Dad?' he said quietly.

For a moment there was no movement. A frozen image. Then slowly the fingers parted their grip and the head turned towards him.

'Dad, it's me.'

'George?' Dad said, as if doubting his words. 'George! Oh my God, it's you!'

He jumped up off the bench and threw his arms around him. George could feel the whole of Dad's body shaking.

'Dad I'm sorry, I'm so sorry.'

'It's OK, everything's OK.' Dad squeezed him tight. 'Oh George I'm just glad you're safe that's all. Nothing else matters now. Just that you're safe. Here let me look at you.' He took a step back.

'Dad,' said George, looking up into his dad's dampening eyes. 'I've found Mum. She's trapped. Trapped in a place called Leesome Shrouds.'

'Oh George,' gasped his dad grabbing the top of George's arms to steady himself. 'Really? Is she really?'

'Yes Dad, *really*,' George smiled. 'I wouldn't lie about something like that would I? She told me to tell you that she misses you loads, and that she loves you.'

'I can't believe it.' Dad turned away for a moment. 'She's alive. After all these years. I knew that she'd gone to Leesome Shrouds that day, but when she didn't come home I just assumed that something terrible must have happened to her there.' He roughly wiped his arm across his face. George saw a tear drop from his chin.

'Why didn't you tell me? I could have gone to look for her.'

'What? And lose you too! And George, you forget, you were so young, I couldn't tell you that she'd gone to another world could I? What if you'd told someone else. Before you'd know it everyone would know. They'd definitely have believed for sure that I'd murdered her then wouldn't they, making up ridiculous tales like that?'

'Suppose.'

'George, how is she? Is she alright?'

'She's fine Dad,' said George, thinking back to his mum's trembling body outside the lift. 'She's just fine.'

Dad turned back around to face him. His face was all wet again, eyes bloodshot and lips quivering. 'That's amazing. *George* isn't this amazing?' He smiled a sad smile.

'Yeah Dad.'

'You see George I wasn't sure if you were old enough to travel Interglobally or not. I mean your mother and I had always said that we wouldn't tell you about the lift until you were 16. But that morning I heard you get up an hour early, and when I went to shout to tell you, something stopped me. I can't tell you how much I've regretted it these last couple of weeks.'

'No need for regret now though.'

'Yeah definitely, no need now. And George, I'm sorry too.'

'What for?'

'For all those missed years with you, I wasn't fair to you. Treating you like that. Ignoring you all the time. You didn't deserve it. I just didn't know what to say, I'm so sorry George.'

'It's OK,' said George quietly, not sure whether it was or not.

'I just believed that she was dead, and I felt so helpless, so useless.'

'I know.'

'Well from now on George things are going to be different. I'm going to be different, and I'm going to make sure we have some quality time together. Catch up on all those lost years eh?' Dad put his arm tightly around him. 'Come on then George let's get you *home*, then you can tell me all about Leesome Shrouds, and maybe we can make a plan of how we're going to get her back here.'

George walked into the house. It smelt musty and damp: funny he'd never noticed it before. He went over to a framed picture hanging on the wall in the hall, Mum and Dad were holding his hand; he was about five. He hadn't looked at it for years, he hadn't been able to. He decided that he would take some photos back to Mum the next time he went to Leesome Shrouds. And somehow deep inside, he believed that there definitely would be a next time. He felt a surge of happiness flood his veins. George smiled, life felt better for him now than it had done in years.